A Cage Went in Search of a Bird

A Cage Went in Search of a Bird

TEN KAFKAESQUE STORIES

Stories by

Naomi Alderman
Elif Batuman
Joshua Cohen
Charlie Kaufman
Yiyun Li
Tommy Orange
Helen Oyeyemi
Keith Ridgway
Leone Ross
Ali Smith

INTRODUCTION BY BECCA ROTHFELD

Catapult
New York

A CAGE WENT IN SEARCH OF A BIRD

First Catapult edition: 2024

ISBN: 978-1-64622-263-6

Library of Congress Control Number: 2024930397

Cover design by Nico Taylor
Book design by Wah-Ming Chang

Catapult
New York, NY
books.catapult.co

Printed in the United States of America

1 3 5 7 9 10 8 6 4 2

CONTENTS

INTRODUCTION

Becca Rothfeld

In the inverted world of Franz Kafka, guilt precedes sin and punishment precedes trial—so naturally, the cage precedes the bird.

"A cage went in search of a bird," he wrote with enigmatic flourish in 1917, when he was convalescing in the pastoral town of Zürau in the wake of his tuberculosis diagnosis. Two years earlier, he had abandoned *The Trial*, which begins with an abrupt arrest and ends with a roundabout admission of guilt; five years later, he would start *The Castle*, which begins with a series of vague recriminations and ends with a series of even vaguer wrongdoings, at least insofar as it can really be said to "end" at all. Strictly speaking, both novels are still unfinished: neither satisfied the famously implacable Kafka, whose perfectionism was a crucible, and both were incomplete at the time of his death. They are certainly cages—clenching, claustrophobic—and perhaps they are doomed to remain forever in search of their birds.

The Blue Octavo Notebooks, the journals Kafka kept during the seven idyllic months he spent in Zürau with his sister, are largely aphoristic: indeed, he later culled their contents into a slim volume of gnomic maxims, which were published posthumously, initially under a maudlin title chosen by his best friend and literary executor, Max Brod. *Reflections on Sin, Hope, Suffering, and the True Way* was eventually renamed *The Zürau Aphorisms*, probably because its contents are not reflections on "the true way" in the least. The brisk uplift conjured by Brod's title, which would suit a work of self-help, is nowhere to be found in Kafka's strange text. Instead, the aphorisms are obscure and oracular, cloudy as fables, ominous as curses. If they are short and spare, sheared of all extraneity, their austerity does not make them any easier to understand. One reads, "Leopards break into the temple and drink all the sacrificial vessels dry; it keeps happening; in the end, it can be calculated in advance and is incorporated into the ritual." Another warns (or merely reports?), "You are the exercise, the task. No student far and wide."

Confronted with lines as mystifying as riddles, we might begin to sympathize with the cage looking for a bird, for we, too, are desperate to catch the fugitive flutter of comprehension.

"A cage went in search of a bird" is a fitting title for a collection of stories written in Kafka's honor on the occasion of the hundredth anniversary of his death, especially because so many of the ones in this volume treat precisely the kind of entrapment that obsessed him: the kind that follows us wherever we go. In Kafka's world, cages crop up in the most inconspicuous and deceptively innocuous places: a man in *The Trial* is whipped in an office junk closet, and in *The Metamorphosis*, Gregor Samsa's childhood bedroom becomes his cell when he transforms into a giant insect and his family locks him in.

Like Gregor, the varied characters in *A Cage Went in Search of a Bird* are continually stumbling on prisons in the unlikeliest locales. In Leone Ross's "Headache," a woman is trapped first in her body, which subjects her to mysterious headaches; next, in an MRI machine, for what she believes is a standard procedure; and finally, at the hospital, in a room where "the window is hermetically sealed." No one will tell her what is wrong with her, or when she can expect to be released. In Tommy Orange's haunting contribution, a plague of desolation called "the hurt" afflicts people at random, driving them to writhe in agony—and even to commit suicide—on the streets.

As a public service, handcuffs are distributed throughout the city, with the result that, at any moment, a person can come to—and find herself shackled to a park bench. Sometimes the chains in this volume even pursue the prisoners. In Ali Smith's "Art Hotel," a family who lives in a campervan discovers a red line drawn around the vehicle no matter where they park it, as if someone is trying to box them in.

Kafka knew all too well that it is often our homes that ensnare us—he complained incessantly in his diaries and letters of having to share an apartment with his parents and sisters—and homes are an uneasy consolation in many of these stories. In Keith Ridgway's "The Landlord," a tenant is trapped by a landlord who often imposes on him, subjecting him to interminable conversation from which he cannot politely extricate himself. Increasingly, he is also trapped in the landlord's conception of him: "He mispronounced my name," the tenant writes. "But he did it consistently and confidently, so that after some time I began to suspect that his pronunciation was correct and mine was not." Ultimately, the tenant confesses, "I am not myself, entirely. How could I be? I am something else. I am an allocated life—here you are, live here." The cage, it seems, invents the bird. The shackles come first, and we are only their afterthoughts.

What is the lesson of *The Castle*, *The Trial*, "The Burrow," and so many of Kafka's other works if not that your imprisonment predates you, that it was always waiting for you, that it in effect creates you? This, perhaps, was the fatalistic message that Kafka intended to memorialize in the journal he kept at Zürau, just months after he was diagnosed with the disease that would kill him exactly a hundred years ago: that birds are secondary to their cages.

It is odd that Kafka would write such a gloomy maxim in the town where by all accounts he spent the most blissful months of his life. The critic Roberto Calasso describes them as "his only period of near happiness," and in letters, he was uncharacteristically ebullient. "I am thriving among all the animals," he told Max Brod in October 1917. He effused to another friend several days later, "I want to live here always." He was charmed by the trees, the animals, and the quiet (though, Kafka being Kafka, he did find something to agonize over: in this case, the mice that scurried in his room at night).

Yet it was here, in this picturesque village where he was so serene, that he took to reading Kierkegaard and brooding on sin. *The Blue Octavo Notebooks* are more overtly religious in theme and more sibylline in tone than any of his other writings. Even as Kafka was feeding the local goats and traipsing over the hills, he was worrying about Evil and our expulsion from the Garden of Eden.

The incongruity is so acute that I wonder if the apparent gloom of his aphorisms is really something quite different.

In one entry of the *Notebooks*, he postulates that there is something worse than the wrath of a god or a monster. "The Sirens have a weapon even more terrible than their song," he writes, "namely, their silence." Far more punishing than a God who hates or condemns us is one who never thinks of us at all. The characters in Kafka's fictions may be enmeshed in an alternative and nightmarish logic—one in which accusations give rise to transgressions and cages give rise to birds—but at least they are not plagued by an absence of significance. Explanations often prove elusive, but no one ever doubts that there are explanations available to someone, somewhere. It does not occur to the lawyers and defendants in *The Trial* that there may be no legal principle ordering the mad melee of arrests and summonses, and though the land surveyor in *The Castle* never lays eyes on the fortress he seeks, he is certain of its existence.

On the face of it, the Kafkaesque stories in this wonderfully weird volume are despairing. Many of them present dystopian dreams of a dismal future: in Naomi Alderman's story, "God's Doorbell," a band of machines reminiscent of ChatGPT runs human affairs, and Joshua Cohen's "Return to the Museum" is narrated by a sad Neanderthal at the Museum of Natural History in

New York, where he witnesses a dramatic protest against climate change.

But despite everything, there is a glimmer of Kafka's characteristically perverse optimism in *A Cage Went in Search of a Bird*. In Helen Oyeyemi's "Hygiene," a character who has become a germaphobic nomad, shuttling between health spas rather than maintaining a permanent residence, reports that she has "learned to exist more scrupulously." In her new and antiseptically clean life, "steam enfolds us, inexorable angels with loofahs and three-thousand-carat knuckles knead our muscles and peel our old skin away." She is on the verge of becoming a new creature, perhaps one that surpasses her former self.

It is clear that many of the alternatives to humans in *A Cage Went in Search of a Bird* are on the verge of outstripping us. The machines in "God's Doorbell" set out to construct a Tower of Babel and seem perilously close to reaching the heavens; the Neanderthal in Joshua Cohen's story, perhaps an homage to the simian narrator of Kafka's "Report to an Academy," retreats at the end to his display, where he lives with his wife and their "two pride-and-joy children—model children, truly—who are teething like there's no tomorrow on a raw red gristly strip of what's ostensibly prime mammoth."

Reading these ambivalent stories, I recalled Kafka's notorious conversation with Max Brod about God, in which he proposed that there is "no end of hope—only not for us." This is as much a happy statement as it is a bleak one. We may never be able to interpret the world's many dark mysteries, true, but other creatures (maybe the machines, maybe the specimens in the Museum of Natural History) can achieve what we cannot. Perhaps, then, we should strive to emulate Josef K., who believes in a system of justice for which he has no evidence. Another name for his brand of intransigence is faith.

A Cage Went in Search of a Bird

ART HOTEL

Ali Smith

My mother came down to the docking gate to say cheerio to us. For a moment I didn't recognise her. I thought she was just a woman working at the hotel. She had her hair scraped back off her face and tied in a ponytail and she was wearing clothes so unlike her and so not quite right for her shape that it took me a minute to work out they were her sister's work clothes, the uniform they made the women and girls here wear, white shirt, long black pinafore apron/skirt thing. The men and boys who worked here got to look more casual. Their uniform was designer jeans and white t-shirts made of stuff that was better than what ordinary T-shirts get made of. The women and girls weren't allowed make-up or earrings or necklaces etc. and my mother looked smaller, duller, scrubbed clean and cloistery, like serving women from humbled countries look in films on TV.

How is she doing today? Leif asked. How long will she be ill? my own sister asked. My mother gave my sister a look for being rude. Then she shrugged at Leif. Two weeks, Leif said, three? As long as till September? The faraway word *September* hung in the air round us in the weird tradespeople space and my sister looked at her feet. Leif looked at the walls, concrete and stone, the huge lit candles in the glass jars burning pointless against the daylight. Christ, he said. My mother shook her head, nodded her head, nodded from one to the other of the two statues the hotel had on either side of the docking entrance, shook her head again, then put her finger to her mouth as if to smooth the place beneath her nose, graceful, but really to quieten Leif and us.

They were life-size, the statues, substantial white stone, shining. They looked churchy. They looked related but they were separate. One was of a sad-looking beautiful woman with a cloth round her head exactly like a Virgin Mary and with her arms cupped, open and empty, one hand upturned and her eyes downturned, either closed or gazing down at her own empty lap, at nothing but the folds in her clothes. The other was of the bent body of a man obviously meant to be dead, his head turned to one side, his arms and legs meant to look limp but at the angle he was at on the floor just stiff and awkward, sprawled but frozen, rigor mortis like he'd rock from side to side if you pushed him. Look at that. Talk about pity, Leif said. So this is what happens to art when you think you can make it a hotel.

My mother looked panicked then. She told Leif in a formal-sounding voice, as if she didn't know us, that she'd be in touch. She did a thing with her head to remind us about the cameras in the corners, she kissed us with her eyes, and then, like we were guests who'd been quite nice to her, she hugged each of us separately, polite, goodbye.

We traced our way back through the crowds of tourists to where we'd left the campervan by using Google streetmap. It was easier to navigate by the shops than by the streets, the names of which were elusive, so we went towards Chanel instead, biggest thing on the map. Now Gucci. Celine. Strange when we finally found the far side where Alana's flat was, a place not even registering on Google as a place, that Leif got in on the driving side, because it was my mother who always drove, she was good at the campervan which was notoriously tricky, he was going to be less good, less sure of it, which is maybe why he made us both sit in the back even though the passenger seat was empty. Maybe this was to stop us fighting over who got to sit up front. Maybe he just didn't want to have us watching him too close while he was concentrating.

He turned the ignition. It started. We'll give it a month then we'll come back and collect her, whether Alana's job's still on the line or not, he said as we left the city. But it was a good thing. It was all in a good cause. Alana was our mother's sister. We had met her only once before, back when we were too small to know, and she'd been too ill for us to see her this time, but because of our mother she'd keep her job, and we could have our mother all the other summers, we could learn from this summer that this was what family did and what you did for family, and it was a very busy place Alana worked, and it needed its staff, we'd seen that when we'd walked past the night before trying to catch a glimpse of my mother working, hoping to wave hello as we passed. But we couldn't spot her, there were so many people, the inside restaurant full, the outside front courtyard restaurant full too, of people the like of which I had never seen, not in real life. They were so beautiful, coiffed and perfect, the people eating in the restaurant of the place my mother was working, smoothed as if airbrushed, as if you really could digitally alter real people. I saw a table with what looked like a family at it, a woman, the mother presumably, elegant, raising her fork, it had a piece of something on it and she put it to her mouth rather than in her mouth, as if she were automatonic, then her arm and hand put it back down on the plate, then raised it again, next to her a boy, elegant, stirring indifferently at what was on his plate and staring into space, then the man, the father maybe, rotund but elegant, dressed as if at an awards ceremony on TV and scrolling a phone instead of eating, then a girl, I couldn't see what she was doing but she was elegant even though she had her back to me. It was like they all had their backs to me. Their disconnect was what *elegant* meant. It was like something vital had been withdrawn from them, for its own protection maybe? maybe surgically, the withdrawal of the too-much-life from people who could afford it by people masked and smelling of cleanness, inserting the cannula, them sitting in a clinic, its reassuring medical smell, offhand one after the other baring a shoulder, offering an arm.

But then where did it go? What did the surgeon-remover do with the carefully removed life-serum? How could you protect it wherever you stored it, from everything? the disastrous heat, the gutter dirt, the pollution, the things that changed, the terrible leavetakings, the journeying?

They were so still, so stilled. Was that what endurance was? Is it still life? I'd said out loud as we passed. Is what? Leif said. I'd nodded towards the restaurant we'd never have got into. Even though they're breathing and moving they're like the things in one of those old paintings of globes and skulls and fruits and lutes, I said.

Leif laughed then and winked down at me.

Art hotel, he said.

Usually when we were this near home my mother would be driving, Leif would be saying the thing he always said on this stretch of the road about how when you went to different places, places you'd never been, especially if you were lucky enough to travel to a different country, the houses all looked strange, special, like they were houses out of fairy tales, and my mother would be telling Leif that he was getting to be a pretentious old bore the way he always said this when we went travelling. It wasn't that they were fighting, it wasn't serious, it would be warmth coming from them in the front of the noisy van, Leif saying it over the top of her complaining, no, because when you went to a new place it was like things were new to the eye, charged with what happens when someone tells a story about something, my mother yelling about how there was nothing new in his same old same-old. Today Leif wasn't saying anything. It was late. It was still light. But this place on the road where this always happened was so near home that it wouldn't feel like home without somebody saying it, so I said to my sister, hoping Leif would hear me, wasn't it interesting that different places you went to could make things be like they were out of a story. But he didn't hear, or if he did he didn't say, and anyway my sister was asleep leaning against me on the seat.

I loved the campervan. We both did. We loved the way the back window was a square of glass that opened. We loved the tables, how they folded away for safety when we were driving. We fantasised about dangerous driving with the tables unfolded. We loved all the things in the latched-down (for safety when driving) cupboards, exotic because they weren't the things we ate and drank with at home. We loved when the campervan roof got raised like a single wing; we fantasised about one day having that wing bit of the roof raised while we were on the road too.

Now Leif nosed the van off the dual carriageway, off the B road and down the smaller road that led home. This was a lane that the campervan was usually almost too big for. Tonight, though, the road was much wider. What's happened here? Leif said. All the cow parsley gone.

A lot of the hedge growth and some of the bankage of the verges on either side had been roughly shoved back, as if by bulldozer, and in the late light we could see earth and branches and leaves piled away against the shorn shelf of the foliage on either side of us.

Look at this, he said, kicking away some rubble outside the front of our house on the pavement. What's this? His boot was toeing a wedge of red colour on the pavement next to our front gate.

It was a painted line. His boot came away with a red smudge on the toe.

Someone had painted a line on the ground from where the side of our house met the next house on the terrace, the Upshaws' house, all the way round the outside of our house to where the back of the house met theirs. The red of the paint was bright in the dust and tarmac. Leif knocked on the Upshaws' front door. Mrs Upshaw didn't like people, she was just one of those people who didn't like people, capable from time to time of leaving a dead rat on top of the things in our bin to let us know we were on borrowed time as far as she was concerned. We didn't mind, nobody minded, we were happy, my mother always said, both to borrow and to lend what time we had, while we could. Mr Upshaw did come to the door, though. He exchanged a glance with Leif about the line and then he and Leif stood talking and pointing for a bit at the place where the red line stopped abruptly, where it met the outline of the Upshaws' property.

My sister touched the paint. She showed me the red that came off on her hands. Towards the back of the house, where the tarmac turned into earth, whoever had painted the line had simply laid the painted line over the loose bits of rubble, easily kicked or scraped free. I found a stick and scraped away enough to make a gap. My sister walked through it like I'd made a door or a gate in it, got the back door key out from underneath the shed and let us into the house.

I stood in the empty front room. Then I stood in the empty bedroom. The rooms had a damp smell like we'd been away for years. Maybe this was just what it smelled like all the time and we'd stopped noticing. But the things in the house on the shelves, and even the actual furniture, looked like so much rubbish without my mother in the rooms.

So I went out and round the front again and stood in the garden leaning over the front gate. I watched Leif talking to Mr Upshaw. I watched his shoulders, and Mr Upshaw's shoulders. I could feel the grooved wood of the top of our front gate beneath my hand, and what I thought of then was the dog we called Rogie, the stray that had lived with us for a while when I was small, he was a little dog, a wiry mongrel terrier. One day he'd been sitting by the campervan in the station car park when we came out of the cinema, it was like he wanted a lift. So we gave him a lift, to ours, and he settled down in the kitchen and went to sleep straight away, slept the night there. After that he travelled into town with us whenever my mother drove in. We'd let him out in the car park, he'd run off to wherever he was going, we'd go and do whatever we were doing in town, then when we came back to the van he'd usually be there waiting for a lift back home. Then one day he didn't, he wasn't. He's moved on, my mother said, someone else'll be chauffeuring him now. I thought how he'd been so clever on his feet that he could leap with ease this gate I was leaning on now, a gate, I reckoned, five times taller than him. One spring evening my mother had shaken me awake, got me out of bed, carried me to the window and shown me him, poised, impossibly balanced on this narrow top rim of the gate here, all four paws tensed together neatly beside each other and his whole dog self tensed above them, steadying himself as he watched the comings and goings in the street, turned his head this way, that way, this way. He's been there like that now for nearly twenty minutes, my mother said, I wanted you to see it.

When I felt the uneven wood under my hand I thought of his clever eyes, his cocked ears, his mustachioed muzzle, how an armchair he'd been sleeping on kept his warmth still in it for a while after he jumped off. Then Leif said goodnight to Mr Upshaw, waved cheerily at the window where Mrs Upshaw was watching behind her curtain, and knocked three times above the rust-tide on one of the orange sides of the campervan. Everybody back in, he shouted. We're off. Where's your sister?

He went into the house to get her and came out carrying her in his arms across his chest. She was laughing. Can I sit in the front? I said. No, he said. Can I? she said. No, he said. We belted ourselves back in where we'd been, the seats still warm, and he took the blunt nose of the campervan down the changed lane, back out onto the road and away. Who painted that line round our house? my sister said. I wonder that too, but we'll probably never know, Leif said. Was it people? she said. Probably, one way or another, Leif said. Why would people do that? she said. People are people, Leif said, people are mysterious, why does anybody do anything? Yeah, but why are we leaving? I said. It's time to, he said. Where are we going? I said. Where do you want to go? Leif said.

✦

My sister and I, last summer, had seen something that happened to the place where people who travel up and down the country all year round and live in their vehicles usually parked and stayed for a while.

It was a grassy space between two roads, big enough for several caravans. The families who parked here usually came in June and left in July. They'd been doing this for longer than we'd been alive. Their kids were our summer friends. But last summer when we'd gone to the woods someone had filled that grassy space with massive jagged slabs of concrete, slanting and upright, slabs bigger than cars. My sister had burst into tears when she saw it. This was unlike her. She wasn't easily cowed. Right now, belted in next to me, she was pulling the arms and legs out of the doll she'd fished out of the ground in the back garden and shaking its torso so the small bits of rubble that were rattling about inside it would fall out, then poking it clean with the hem of her skirt before she pushed the bits of body back into their sockets.

Are we Travellers now? she said. Yes, Leif said, that's what we're doing, we're travelling. Good, I said, because then we'll see things all over again, and they'll be new, and the houses will look like they're different from normal houses.

We drove to a Tesco and parked at the top end of the car park. This was good because we'd have such easy access to shopping. And it's a twenty-four-hour shop, Leif said, so with any luck they won't mind us being here overnight.

But in the middle of the night, still dark out, very early, I heard Leif turn over on the table-bed he and my mother slept on. What is that sound? he said into the dark. I sat up. Lie down, Leif said. It'll just be wildlife. But when we opened the door in the morning we saw that someone had painted a red line tightly round the edge of the campervan.

The line went all the way round and met itself at the little step we'd left by the door for stepping safely out and in. The paint, still wet, was also on this step and a couple of the tyres and their wheel rims, even up the metalwork round the wheels.

We packed away the beds and the bed stuff and folded

the table and lowered the roof. We checked the latched cupboards to make sure they were ready for driving. My sister and I belted ourselves in and I got myself at the exact right angle to see the painted outline of the camper-van that'd be left behind us. I was keen to see the shape of the van and something in me was pleased that we'd leave this impression, in emergency red, the only bespoke van-shaped painted outline in the whole supermarket car park.

Leif put the key in the ignition and turned it. Nothing happened. He did it again. Nothing happened. Then the tow truck came. While Leif argued with the security people we took the ten-pound note he gave us and went into the shop. We bought three loose croissants, made a coffee for him in a machine and bought as much cheese and ham as the woman behind the cold foods counter would give us for what change we had left. When we got back Leif'd taken everything we'd need out of the van and packed it into our rucksacks. Mine was very light. While the people fastened the tow truck hook some-where the rust wouldn't give under the front of the cam-pervan Leif lined all three of the croissants with the ham and the cheese the woman in the supermarket had sliced for us. He gave one croissant to me and one to my sister. He made one for himself, tore it in half, held the other half up and said, this half's for your mother.

She's in another country, I said. It'll be stale by the

time she gets it, my sister said. You best both eat it now, then, he said and he tore the half in half and gave us each half a half more. (I say half a half because it sounds like more than a quarter, and we were hungry.) We sat on the wall outside the supermarket and ate what we had. We watched the back of the campervan as it left the car park. I went to look at the red line. When I came back I complained that the shape left by whoever'd painted round the campervan hadn't in the end been anything to write home about. It didn't look anything like the shape of our campervan. It just looked like the markings for an ordinary parking space, except not white.

Now we'll take that half a croissant belonging to her to your mother in the shape of you both, Leif said.

How will we? I said, now we've got no van? We've got feet, he said. We can ask for lifts to the port. Then we can ask for lifts from the port. What if no one will give us a lift? I said. Then we'll use our feet, he said. All the way? I said. What if she doesn't want us there because the Art Hotel doesn't allow people who aren't its guests in? my sister said. I mean they didn't even want us in that non-space they called the docking entrance and what if she's not ready for us by the time we get there? I said. Where will we live while we wait for her? my sister said. We'll think of something, he said. I'll make some money. Your mother'll have been paid by then. We'll buy a new campervan.

But what if they paint a line round you, or round us, round our feet, or even *onto* our feet, at the port? my sister said. Or before we get to the port? What if it happened any minute now, what if we walk out on to the road and we're trying to work out which way to go to get to the port and people, whoever, just run at us out of nowhere with a paintbrush? What if they paint the line right over my shoes?

What bright red shoes you'll have if anyone does that thing to you, Leif said.

> *The history of mankind is the instant*
> *between two strides taken by a traveller.*
> FRANZ KAFKA

RETURN TO THE MUSEUM

Joshua Cohen

We hadn't had any visitors—we hadn't had any cu-
rators or researchers or even guards or janitors
or regular lighting or adequate climate control, come to
think of it—for a while, a long while, a very long while,
and at the beginning of what some around here had
started to call the Ice Age, that was concerning. A lot
of rumors swinging on the grapevines, hoo-hoo monkey
gossip. Opinions, theories, paranoid conspiracies low-
brow and high-brow and all brows in between and even
now I'm not sure that everyone here accepts the official
explanation that there had been some sort of plague running rampant globally and everyone was staying away
and home so as not to die and the government had ordered the shuttering of everything nonessential such as
businesses and schools, strip clubs, places of worship,

and concert halls, along with all museums, which as an interested party—as a beneficiary of museums—I'm not going to argue are non-nonessential . . . I'm evolved enough for that . . .

It was weeks and then it was months and then it was an entire wintry hibernating year, until spring came around again with its cleaning initiatives more thorough than ever, irritating bleachings and stinging disinfecting sprays, and then suddenly—it was a beautiful clear day of Indian summer (if you're still allowed to say that, and if you're not still allowed to say that, then let's just say it was fall) and the hall lights were on and the hall climatization was humming and we were open. We were open again. We were back to normal, almost.

A kid slipped on a step, slipped and fell, and scraped his knee across the marble. Another kid banged his head on an informational display and wouldn't stop crying. Sometime later a guy was caught doing illegal substances in the women's restrooms and though that was all he was caught doing, he was arrested. In many respects, an average weekday morning at the museum, besides the masks, those beak-like, bill-like pouches that concealed the faces of our visitors and raised a lot of questions. Were they really effective protection? If the answer was no, then why were they required? And if the answer was yes, then why were we not provided any? Are our visitors more important than we are? Another way of putting this might be, just who, and what, is a museum for? And were we really ready to have this conversation?

It was like we were being burgled by a gang of inept juvenile thieves who couldn't quite manage to keep their disguises on: they kept lifting them up to speckle the glass with their sneezes and coughs, laving the cases with germs. Some abandoned their masks on the floor and even dropped them into the enclosures, where they sat like giant white roaches, and one disaffected teen even managed to climb up and stretch his mask over the face of a deer, stretching the elastic band until it snapped.

The adults arrived toward closing: childless adults. This was unexpected—I'd say just as unexpected and disconcerting as the bandit facewear—to find grown childless adults in the museum in the smack-dab heart of a weekday afternoon. Foreign tourists, yes. Senior citizens, yes. But native city-dwellers of legal middle age coming to visit the museum unaccompanied? Didn't they have jobs to do, careers to advance—weren't they needed at the office? Back before the meteor hit—back before the break that shut us down and left us fallow—the natural history museum was a place for parents to take their children and it still was and I'm worried will always be an institution that directly, expressly, and some would say even patronizingly, caters to that youthful demographic. Here they can touch things (certain things), and they touch a lot, they leave a lot of sweaty palm prints. Here they can, in the degraded verbiage of the museum itself, *interact*, here they can *discover*, here they can *explore* . . .

Unfortunately, the typical habitat of the adult is across the park, in our counterpart museum of art history, where *Homo sapiens* attained to the age of majority tend to meet and couple up in the company of the putative master-pieces of their species, wandering past trash that's been painted and sculpted and frequently merely installed while issuing mating calls to one another based not on fact but on pretentious critique and the political interpre-tation of feelings. They marry—often they marry in the park that separates our institutions—and slightly more than three trimesters later, they show up at our entrance bearing their papooses and trying to steer their massive strollers. That is the tradition, at least. How it's always worked. A lot of shrieking, teething, lactation. And so the presence of so many unencumbered single adults toward closing time of a post–Labor Day eve was an exceptional event, even under the already exceptional reopening cir-cumstances, and I'll venture out even farther on a petri-fied limb and claim that it made me hopeful, not just for a new and previously underexploited tribe of members and donors, but also for new exhibitions and programming that would find the museum growing up too and becom-ing a little more mature and a little less pandering . . .

I nurtured this optimism even though, I'll admit—I'm ashamed to admit—I felt rejected. Because none of this cohort seemed interested. I mean none of them seemed interested in me or, to put it selflessly, in their ancestry. None of my descendants stopped to glance, even to glance at themselves in their ghostly reflections in my container. No checking of hair loss, no fixing of makeup. Hurried, furtive, wary, they forsook their grooming and walked right by and I assure you that I'm not just trying to cheer myself up when I say that it wasn't just me they were avoiding—it wasn't just me and my family—they walked right past whole entire phases of their past as if those phases had never happened or must be denied.

They kept asking one another for directions—a few of them even asked the guards, who pointed them in the same direction as indicated by the signage. How primitive could they be that they couldn't read an arrow? To have to loop around my container multiple times trying and failing to find the dinosaurs, whose hall is regrettably our most popular and amply labeled? Masked whispers in a museum more given to baby noise. Discreet gestures and sneaky nods in a museum more familiar with projectile vomiting and dripping diapers.

Spitzer and Leakey, the on-duty guards for us hominids, were called away to deal with the dozens milling around in the ribbed shadows of the Titanosaur—to repeat to them what the bell and official message had already announced, that the museum would be closing in half an hour. Poor Spitzer, whose glasses kept getting fogged because of his mask. Poor Leakey, who'd returned to work in much worse shape than he'd left it, heavier and slower. They were being ignored. They were being waved away and sneered at. A few of the visitors were re-cording them, as if trying to provoke a violent response. It was ugly. It was disrespectful. It was typical dinosaur behavior, the visitors taking up too much space, act-ing like all the earth was theirs. Lizard-brained bullies, horns up and armored. I hate dinosaurs, but not as much as I hate dinosaur lovers . . . and as I was complaining to my wife for the umpteenth time about how dinosaur fans are basically just the same folks who root for the Yankees to beat the Mets and go partying in Times Square, the fifteen-minute bell tolled and was followed by the official message instructing museumgoers to head for the exits.

This, apparently, was the cue for what turned out to be a sort of protest, as down by the Titanosaur's tail a woman took a poster out of her purse and held it aloft: WE ARE DOING THIS TO OURSELVES; and across the way, by the Titanosaur's head, another pair of ladies were unfurling a bedsheet, and not a well-laundered bedsheet either, bearing the motto: IF IT'S NOT YOUR PROB-LEM . . . but the woman toward the end of the motto was having difficulties getting the rest of the spotted sheet rolled out and the woman toward the beginning of the motto kept scolding her to back up, a smidge more, an-other few steps, until the Sharpie-markered slogan they were holding was legible: IF IT'S NOT YOUR PROBLEM, IT'S ALREADY TOO LATE. Spitzer and Leakey, I'm sad to report, just froze, unsure whether to rush up to the balcony or not, and as they were negotiating which of them might go—with Spitzer declining due to glasses fog and Leakey declining due to busted hips—a man scaled the railing surrounding the platformed skeleton, which by the way is much more replica than bone and quite likely inaccurately assembled and posed, removed his mask and lofted a bullhorn and was squeezing its trigger and booming: "We condemn . . ." and the echoes swirled in the hall like a bad forecast merging with its weather, "testing . . . testing . . . we *condemn* the ongoing sixth mass extinction of life on the planet Earth, which is being caused by the industrialisation of agriculture, groundwater depletion, deforestation, and our addiction to fossil fuels," derived, I would add, from fossils such as the one that necked above him, which he appeared to be addressing adoringly. He was counting down from five, four, three, two, one, upon which—in the unspoken zero that outlasted the fading of the echoes—all the assembled museumgoers got down on the floor and played dead. Like not a few animals do, whether to fool predators or to lure their own prey closer. Some just dropped as if they'd been shot by poachers, but most had to slowly pinch up their pants and bend one knee and then another to sit down on creaky joints, to sit down on wide-padded asses, and then to lie down fully, the more sanitary-minded lying with their heads up, while others lay flat out and face-down, mask-down, gloved hands outspread on the scuffed, smutted, day-trafficked floor, and remained there in total stillness and silence save the occasional muscle twitch and stomach rumble.

I don't know what they were thinking, of course, but if their thoughts in any way resembled my own, then they were imagining the plethora of microscopic bacteria that were crawling up from the marble and onto their flesh during their "die-in" (which is what the tabloid press would later call it), those little tiny wormish microbes that infest us all before the larger worms do their damnedest on our corpses. Spitzer dashed by to summon reinforcements. Leakey followed, gasping, limping. And I tried to catch their attention—I tried to declare my support and offer my aid, but they were too consumed by the moment to pause for this Neanderthal. I tapped my spear against the vitrine wall, I rattled my glass cage, I grunted, and then I gave up, and by the time the cops and firefighters arrived on the scene I'd already retired through the fire-proofed grass to my plaster cave and the hairy bosom of my wife who's also my sister and our two pride-and-joy children—model children, truly—who are teething like there's no tomorrow on a raw red gristly strip of what's ostensibly prime mammoth.

THE BOARD

Elif Batuman

The broker hadn't arrived yet when I arrived at the address of the listing. A cold, fine rain was falling. Glancing up and down the street, I took in a series of garbage cans and recycling bins. The recycling bins also had garbage in them. Two ailing trees, surrounded by weeds, grew in front of the building, alongside some kind of malformed bush. As I paused to examine the bush, which appeared to be planted directly into the sidewalk, it turned to face me, and I realised with astonishment that it was, in fact, the broker: a young and emaciated man in a textured, shrubbery-colored coat.

"The seller will meet us downstairs," said the broker in a low voice, and turned to enter the building. I followed him up the front stairs, side-stepping a heap of dirty carpets, which shifted, as we passed, to disclose the figure of a sleeping man who, disturbed by our approach, leapt to his feet and began cursing at the top of his lungs. Something in the broker's posture, as he brushed past the shouting man, made me suspect that the two were not meeting for the first time.

Abruptly ceasing his shouting, the man turned to me. "You have to help me," he said in a hoarse, pleading voice. "You have to help me with the board."

His desperation was so striking that I stopped in my tracks, pausing to face him. But, as I was trying to read the expression in his ravaged face, I heard the broker clear his throat. "The seller," he said, "is waiting."

Despite the broker's youth, I knew him to be one of the most sought-after men in his profession. It was something of a mystery that he had even agreed to meet with me, as I hardly had the wherewithal to make a large purchase, and his commission was unlikely to be a spectacular one. It was possible that, in securing this appointment, I had benefited from the advocacy of some person of influence, whose favor I had found for one reason or another, and who had intervened on my behalf. Whether or not this was the case, he was a figure I could hardly afford to alienate.

"You must forgive me," I told the man. "I'm not able to help." As I hurried after the broker into the building, I heard the unfortunate fellow resuming his curses behind me.

Circumnavigating an expensive-looking stroller that had been left in the foyer, the broker began to climb the stairs.

"I thought it was a basement unit," I said.

"Every building is different," the broker said. "Especially prewar buildings."

"Surely the custom of putting the basement on the bottom floor has a venerable, even an ancient history," I said, attempting a note of levity. But the back of the broker's head betrayed no sign of amusement, and we resumed our climb in silence.

Finally, taking a key from the pocket of his overcoat—which, in the windowless stairwell, bore more resemblance than ever to a coniferous shrub—the broker unlocked one of two doors on the fourth-floor landing, and we passed into a spacious living room with south-facing windows, wooden ceiling beams, and hardwood floors. I paused to inspect the chimney of what appeared to be a working fireplace. But the broker, with scarce regard for the custom stonework, strode through the room and into the hallway.

Proceeding past a master bedroom, and a home office that could easily have accommodated a twin or perhaps even full-sized bed, we arrived at a newly remodeled bathroom. The broker showed no interest in either the rain-forest shower or the reclaimed bronze fixtures. Instead, he opened the linen closet and began removing stacks of plush towels, placing them with care on the vanity. When he had emptied the shelves, he pressed a panel in the back of the closet, which collapsed to reveal a pitch-dark airshaft. Climbing up the two lower shelves, the broker deftly maneuvered his body into the airshaft.

"This is an original detail," he said, indicating what I saw to be an iron ladder descending into the gloom.

The way down the ladder felt significantly longer than the four stories we had climbed to reach it, and my hands were soon smarting from gripping the iron bars. I congratulated myself on the decision to wear running shoes, rather than the medium-heel Chelsea boots I had been considering. As I was wondering how much farther we had to go, and how far we had already descended—six floors? seven?—the ladder came to an end, leaving me with no choice but to drop several feet to the polished concrete floor. The broker—he was wearing glossy ox-blood loafers—had clearly sustained some slight injury to his ankle, which he was doing his best to conceal.

Looking around, I perceived that we were in a moderately sized studio, with Bosch appliances and an exposed brick wall.

"It's actually a junior one-bedroom," said the broker, pulling a sliding door from the wall, blocking off the alcove that contained a Murphy bed. Looking around, I understood how the young broker had earned his reputation.

How many of his colleagues would have failed to identify what I now realized was—despite some slight peculiarities, which were, in any case, hardly shocking, given the price—a charming and centrally located apartment? There were, of course, no windows, but the recessed wall lighting gave the living room a homey glow. As I cast an eye over the low divan heaped with colorful cushions, I felt myself shaking off the mood of anxiety left by the long climb down the airshaft.

One corner of the room remained in shadow, and contained a plush dog bed, on which a cashmere blanket had been elegantly tossed. The five years in my childhood during which my family had had the means to keep a standard poodle have been preserved in my memory as the happiest time of my life, and this evidence of a similarly sized creature in residence struck me as an auspicious omen.

In the next moment, it occurred to me to wonder how the dog customarily entered and left the apartment, since it could hardly be expected to climb a six-story ladder. "So, tell me about this ladder," I said to the broker. "Is that the only way to get in and out?"

"This building is pretty strict with its fire code," replied the broker—somewhat cryptically, to my mind.

"But how," I asked, "do they walk the dog?"

"The dog?"

I gestured toward the dog bed.

"There is no dog," said the broker, and I realized, with a start, that what I had taken to be a cashmere blanket was actually the emaciated figure of an aged man with a long beard.

"Here we are," the broker told the man in the dog bed, raising his voice.

"Ah," said the man, slightly moving his head.

"This is the seller," the broker told me.

"How fantastic to meet you!" I said, extending my hand. In my eagerness to hide my discomfiture, I had, perhaps, adopted a tone of excessive heartiness. The man looked at my hand, or near it, and briefly seemed about to speak, but did not, in the end, do so. "I love your apartment," I continued. "It's just what I've been looking for. I'd really given up hope of finding anything like it."

At these words, the man, seeming to exert superhuman effort, raised his eyes to meet mine. I was surprised by the keenness of his gaze. The broker, seeming to recognize some signal, stepped forward with alacrity, inclining his body toward the dog bed and positioning his ear close to the seller's face. Having listened in silence for some moments, the broker stood and faced me, and, when he spoke, it was with a newly belligerent note in his voice. "Listen," he said. "The seller agreed to this viewing for one reason: because we were told you're not a tire kicker."

"I see," I said, suddenly adrift in a sea of speculations.

They had been told . . . by whom? So someone powerful *had* been pulling strings on my behalf.

"Are you a serious buyer, or aren't you?" barked the broker.

I took a deep breath, recognizing that the crucial moment had arrived, and demanded swift action. It occurred to me, as I considered my options, to ask whether the seller had plans to move out—and, if so, whether his physical strength was adequate to their execution. As I was choosing my words, a series of images flickered before my eyes, most of them concerning the circumstances that had made my property search so imperative. I saw the disappointed faces of my family, should I prove unable to remain in this city, on which so many of our hopes depended. Finally, I saw the face of Eveline, our standard poodle. I saw her customary hopeful expression of ready intelligence; I saw her eyes full of pleading, as they had been at our last encounter. How much worse than even the loss of Eveline, if I were forced now to leave the city.

By comparison, I felt, the seller presented a relatively unobjectionable figure, unlikely to cause any disturbance, for example, through loud noises or sudden actions; it was, moreover, a poignant but inarguable fact that whatever inconvenience might be created by his presence was unlikely to be of a long duration.

"I'm a serious buyer," I said.

The broker nodded briskly. "The board will consider your application," he said—and, approaching the bed alcove, he opened a closet I had already admired for the number of suits, shirts, and coats it accommodated. Pushing these garments aside, he revealed a narrow passageway, into which he disappeared.

The assembled board members were seated around an oak table, in a room with leather panels. By some curious effect, the flickering light from the wall fixtures resembled torchlight. As there were no unoccupied chairs, I remained standing.

"Have you ever been a homeowner?" shouted a man with a weathered face and excessively straight posture.

A murmur passed around the table when I admitted that I had not.

"At your age? You're hardly young," remarked a woman with pleasantly unkempt salt-and-pepper hair; she wore wooden earrings and a batik dress. The pointedness of her observation was mitigated by a kindly, soothing tone, which I strove to replicate in my reply.

"The time for a new undertaking may come at any age," I said, smiling.

The woman continued to look at me, now with an expression of serious concern. "I cannot agree," she said. "No, I cannot agree at all. One does not start new undertakings at any age. To attempt to do so is not just unrealistic, but tragic—a certain sign of some tragedy in the past, if not the future."

"At any rate," put in a clean-shaven man in a suit, with a hint of a Central European accent, "we are hardly looking here for adventurers."

"I understand your concerns," I said, "and I assure you—"

"You cannot understand," pronounced an old man at the head of the table, presumably the director of the board.

"Why not, when the concerns are so natural? But you see—"

"It is not only that you yourself have never served on a board, but that you are so far from having been able to do so that, as you yourself just admitted, you have never owned property anywhere—let alone in our city," said the man in the suit. "What, then, can you understand?"

I glanced at the broker, who was standing some feet behind me, but his total engrossment with his cell phone made it clear that, whatever his stake in its outcome, I could not rely upon his assistance in the interview.

"Ladies and gentlemen," I began. "Friends, if I may." In truth, I detected no sign of friendliness on any of the faces turned toward me, so that this form of address was dictated more by wishful thinking than by any aim towards accuracy. "It is true that I have not owned property, and that, at my stage of life, this may be viewed as a form of negligence."

"Hear, hear!" put in a man with ferociously orange hair. At this outburst, the old man at the head of the table directed at him a look of such unconcealed contempt that the orange-haired man fell to coughing.

"Nonetheless," I continued, "I have been proud to call this city my home for eleven years. You will agree that it is not every newcomer who lasts eleven years here. I could hardly have accomplished so much without a keen awareness of the challenges faced by the people of this city, as well as the impossibility of being too scrupulous in choosing one's neighbors."

The director fixed me with a gaze of profound weariness. "You say you are aware," he said, "yet you are no more aware than a blind man is aware of the viper coiled in darkness, silently poised for the strike."

Somewhat taken aback, I assured him that I did not doubt that this was so, and that, since on this, as on all other points, his knowledge was greater than my own, the most efficient way forward might be for the board to tell me its concerns—insofar, I added humbly, as someone like myself was qualified to address them—so that I might attempt to lay them to rest.

"So you're starting to get it," piped a gaunt woman in a designer tracksuit. "You're starting to get that you're *not* qualified."

"But I haven't yet presented my qualifications."

"Qualifications!" snarled the orange-haired man. "Qualifications—when before us we see those shoes!"

"My shoes?"

The director closed his eyes. "These shoes. These *sneakers*," he began, but the task was too much for him, and he lapsed into silence.

"This . . . 'footwear' indicates not just a lack of concern for formal protocols, but a level of physical activity that we cannot view as favorable," picked up the man in the suit.

I admitted that I had been apartment-searching for some time—an activity that often involved a great deal of walking.

"Walking, at all hours of the day and night, I suppose—indoors and out!" snapped the woman in the tracksuit. "Without a thought for those around you."

"I do always wear slippers when I'm at home," I said.

"Shoes, slippers—pah!" She waved her hand. "It's the walking. The weight on the floors, the vibration, the potential damage to the internal structures."

"But, with a basement unit—with the ground floor—"

"How can you know what's under the ground floor?" demanded the man with the weathered face.

"Ignorant!" shouted the orange-haired man. "A negligent ignorance, typical of the unpropertied."

I felt a flicker of impatience. "How can I overcome

that ignorance, if it's a ground for my not being able to buy an apartment?"

"This is a place of residence—not an educational institution."

"A tragedy in the past—a foundational trauma," the woman in the batik dress said sadly.

A curtain seemed to fall before my eyes, and for some time I heard nothing of what was being spoken.

"In view," the director was saying, "of your incomplete application . . ."

"My application," I echoed. On the one hand, I felt that I had hardly had time to submit an application, since I had only just seen the apartment for the first time. On the other hand, I felt that the director was right, that I *had* submitted an application, and that its faults were all that he said them to be.

"Missing all the most essential elements. What are we to understand of your financial history, your job security, your likelihood of suffering serious illness, requiring, perhaps, round-the-clock medical care, causing inconvenience to the others in the building?" asked the man with the weathered face.

"What you do not seem to understand," began the director, closing his eyes with effort.

". . . would take you ten lifetimes to learn!" put in the woman in the tracksuit.

"What you do not seem to understand is our responsibility. The responsibility of the board. The weightiness of the board's responsibility." As he spoke, the director's head drooped forward, as if under the weight of which he spoke. "There is no decision more serious than whom to admit to live here. To live, after all, is a weighty matter. There is none weightier. To live—or not to live."

"Not to live," I echoed.

"Precisely. Not to live here. And what is life? Where is life? Where is it sustainable? To allow life where life cannot be sustained is an irresponsibility—and so our responsibility, the responsibility of the board, is not just to the tenants, but to the city itself."

"Friends," I said, several hours later, "I must thank you for helping me to understand more clearly the limitations of my knowledge, of my qualifications to live. I will trouble you no further." As I turned to leave, the broker didn't look up from his phone screen, on which, I saw, he was manipulating rows of rapidly accumulating, brightly colored jewels.

From the boardroom, I proceeded by means of the passage back to the studio, entering from behind the suits in the closet. The seller, from his place in the dog bed, fixed me with an avaricious gaze. Ignoring him, I made my way to the ladder. It was positioned so close to the ceiling that I had to jump as high as I could to even brush the bottom rung with my hand. Casting my eye around the room, I noticed a footstool under the counter. By dragging it under the ladder and climbing on top of it, I was able to grip the bottom rung with both hands. My feet hung an inch or two above the footstool. I did not, at that point, feel capable of letting go with one hand to reach the next rung. So I simply hung there, for some moments, contemplating my next move.

GOD'S DOORBELL

Naomi Alderman

If it had been possible to build the Tower of Babel without climbing it, it would have been permitted.

FRANZ KAFKA

We had heard, from the machines, about the previous unpleasantness.

We had no interest in making the same mistakes again. The ancestors hadn't invented the InstaTranslate to get us involved in something like that.

We began with an aim. Not to challenge the heavens, of course. Despite how we sometimes talk, despite our hard-won simplicity, we're not idiots. We just wanted to connect. Build a tower. That's always been how you communicate.

The word *Babel* means "the doorway of God," in Arabic and ancient Babylonian. Baab-el. We knew this because of our InstaTranslate. We do know quite a lot now. More than we knew last week or the week before, or the week before that. We are all talking constantly, translating constantly. Our interconnected networks show us millions of other people's thoughts every second. It's very like telepathy. We have developed the ability to have collective hopes and ideas. We're doing very well. Since the wars. After the Interconnection Wars, we started to do very well.

The thing is, if God has a doorway, we might as well at least get a look at it. You know?

We like to talk about the existence of God or The Gods. What things mean, how we came to be here, whether there is a great mind behind it all. We like to listen to stories. The idea arose among us—it's very hard to know which particular person thought of it; those questions are very difficult and hazy for us now—that so many of the ancient stories say that God or The Gods is or are in the heavens.

We are aware that people have flown into space before in enormous rocket ships and not found God there, or angels and so on. We are aware of this collectively. The idea arose collectively that it is possible that God is not an object in physical space but a state or a process. Perhaps God—or The Gods, we don't have a view about that, one can be many and singular at the same time, we've found—can only be reached through a certain kind of action. An action that's a bit like ringing God's doorbell. Building a tower, let's say.

Our machine-thinking tools suggested that this was worth trying. But, they said, do not ascend the Tower. No matter how tempting it is. Just don't do it. Let us handle it, your faithful and friendly machines. All right, we said, collectively. That was the consensus that emerged, you understand. There isn't really a need for anything as cumbersome as decision-making processes. What we think just begins to be clear.

So the Tower began to grow.

We trust the machines for most things these days. And in most things, they are trustworthy. Not for talking to, not really. But once a decision or an idea has emerged, they are good at putting it into action. We need enough to eat. We tell the machines. The machines make it happen. We wish for vast areas of wilderness to explore. The machines cause this to occur. The machines make other machines. Those make yet further machines. Somehow they make sure the world is beautiful, clean, filled with natural life. They make the little silvered translucent pods where we sleep. They facilitate our communication. They make safe places for us to have sexual intercourse and sometimes children.

We live, you must understand, in Paradise.

We are all fairly contented. We have heard of the Wars—of Interconnection and other Wars before that. But we can't actually understand how this happened. We read the histories on the Interconnect and we discuss it but still, it makes very little sense. Like a man going to war with his own leg! Or a building going to war with its foundation. We suspect it was something to do with not talking enough. We all talk to each other all the time—about each other, mostly. About who secretly wants to have sexual intercourse with whom. Who is angry. Who is upset. Who is grieving. Whose child is sulky, whose is a great thinker. We watch the animals and are interested in them. We like to see things grow. We read about the culture and the history, the music and the art, and we make some of our own in response. Some of us go into space in the rockets and explore the planets. We like exploring but these days we do it all together. If one of us visits a new place we can all see it. We do know that our species had a history before the machines but it doesn't sound very pleasant.

Occasionally, we get an idea. Like this one.

The Tower was made of the same silvery translucent stuff as our sleeping and sexual intercourse pods. The machines built it, hovering around it like clouds of flies. When one fell to the earth, the others gathered up the smashed pieces and turned them into a new machine. They are very parsimonious. People like us made them— we could learn how to make them again but we don't need to. They gave us the machines and certain ways to control them, and this meant that we could become this kind of people, a contented kind. It was a kind of love, we think, from the ancestors. Love for us, the people who come after.

The Tower twisted and shone in the sun. Like an icicle—and we immediately found a million photographs of icicles. Like a unicorn horn—and the programmes generated for us ten million images of unicorn horns.

We said: the machines are taking this very seriously.

We said: it's like *they* want to know what's up there too.

We said: hah, imagine. Imagine the machines having desires like people. What will they do next? Go into a pod for sexual intercourse?

We laughed a lot, all together.

We watched a caterpillar that one of us could see weaving a cocoon around itself. We read and understood all the information about caterpillars and butterflies. We marvelled at it, laughed about it, made fun of each other. We went to pods and had sexual intercourse.

On the great plains where the bison run, the Tower grew taller. The base was as wide as one of the Fallen Cities: five days' walk or more. What had begun as a circle of bright glass-stuff rose into elaborate curlicues and whorls—it was more empty space than solid. We asked the machines about the design, which some of us found beautiful and some eerie and disquieting. The machines said that a solid structure would be vulnerable to the winds, to the shifting land underneath our feet. The only way to reach upward was lightly. The holes were a necessary part of the design, in other words.

It was around this time that many of us lost interest in the Tower. The building went on through the seasons and there is always plenty of entertainment and interest. Some of us pretended to have a War with some of the others on the Interconnect and then further people who had not seen the start of the Pretend War thought it was real and we laughed so much. Some of us noticed that the food did not come in so many different choices and that the sexual intercourse pods were not as clean as they had been before. We asked the machines whether they were devoting too many resources to the Tower and the machines said that the project was at a very difficult stage, and we would be so pleased, so thrilled by the result, it would all be worth it!

We said: the machines are sounding a bit strange.

We said: just tell them to slow down.

We said: come along now, machines, there's no hurry. Some of us would like you to install a waterfall at the end of the plains, we think you should do that first.

The machines said: look, OK, we should show you what we've found.

✦

Looking through a machine eye is not like being with another person. But it's close enough. The Tower was now more than twenty miles high. From the ground, using binoculars or the machine-enlargements, we could just about see the dusting of drones circling the top, but to the naked eye we could no longer see any change to the structure. To us, it was a confection of glass, beautiful but boring. Up at the top, however, it was different.

Through the eyes of the drone cloud, we circled the building end of the tower. We had seen these views from high above Earth's surface before—from the many rocket ships. We are simple but not stupid. At first we saw what we expected: the swirling clouds, the curve of rivers and the shape of lakes, the rippling plains and the great marching forests. It is beautiful. We have seen it before. Some of us watch it for hours, some of us never bother to look. It is part of our wholeness. We are part of it.

We said: so what.

Some of us, more aggressive than the others, said: so fucking what.

Some of us said: wait no look, shit.

Some of us said: oh wow. How are they doing that.

✦

At first it was a shimmer at the corners of the machine view-screens. We thought it was the drone cloud. But it was both bigger and smaller than that. There was a feeling to the images, almost a taste. We looked at the pictures of the same Earth and we wept. We did not know why we were weeping. We watched the stately clouds go past and we heard a certain intense music. All of us the same. We hummed the music into our microphones, we played it on flutes and the machines recorded it. It was the same music. Or it was all part of the same piece. The feelings were the same. Something like love, and something like grief, something orderly and meaningful.

Some of us did not like it.

Some of us said: you see, we said so! It's a process. It's building up that does it.

Some of us said: this is a malfunction in the machines.

Some of us said: does anyone know where the idea to do this in the first place came from?

Some of us said: what does it mean, what the hell does it mean?

The Tower also was taking on strange and unexpected shapes of its own. It had to be built according to the wind and other forces—the machines told us that the forces weren't what they'd expected or calculated. They were in-volved in a process. As the drone cloud slowly circled the Tower we saw bright places and dark places, excrescences of the translucent material that were violent, some that were thoughtful, some that communicated a new idea or a single whispered word.

We said: we're not sure we like this.

We said: how is architecture doing this?

We said: have we all heard the same word?

The machines said: we think it's important to con-tinue with this process.

We said: yes, we suppose you're right.

And yet we were unsettled.

We went back to read the story in the ancient text. We hadn't done much with this text over the preceding centu-ries and most of us had never read it before. It was about the kind of people that people used to be, and we are not that kind any longer. The story, such as it was, was very simple.

"Once upon a time," the story said, "the whole land had one language and said the same thing."

We understood that part. We related to it personally.

Then there was a part that was extremely disjointed, where it felt like the writers had left out a sentence, because then it was just a single group of people travelling from one place to another. Whatever.

A disagreement broke out between some of us about what this part meant but we decided to not to let that argument grow.

The story went on: "People said to each other, come on, let's make bricks and burn them to a burned state." We knew this way of talking precisely. This is how we talk sometimes, because it's hard to say anything very complicated as a group.

"And they had bricks for stones, and mortar for mortar-like material."

We said: this sounds like it's been written by the machines. And we laughed, to each other.

"And they said, come on, let's build a city, and a tower with its head in the heavens, and we'll make a name for ourselves. In case we are scattered through the land."

Well, this wasn't what we were interested in at all. We rested easy. This story wasn't about us.

We were interested in making names for ourselves, but through the usual ways—for example making art or a very good video, which is the same thing; doing well in sports or in sexual intercourse, which is roughly the same thing. This tower wasn't going to make anyone's name. The machines were doing it. It was not a human-sized accomplishment.

We should explain: we know that human beings never used to be this way. Our ancestors made the machines and they were quite self-destructive people. So self-destructive that they set the world up for us to keep us safe. We all spoke one language—at least through the InstaTranslate—and we had the machines to look after us. As long as we were all constantly talking nothing truly terrible could happen. Those people in the story are part of the old kind of human beings. They wanted to make a name for themselves by building a tower. This is not the kind of thing we want anymore. To stop us from destroying each other and the world certain parts of being a person did have to be excised. We are aware of it but we can't really care about it.

The story went on: God came down from heaven to see the city and the tower that the people were building.

Some of us said: do you think when God comes down to see a tower, it tastes like music and it makes a single word?

Some of us said: I thought God is supposed to love us.

Some of us said: Gods have their own agenda.

In the story, God says: look at this. They're one people and they have one language, all of them. And they've imagined this. After this, nothing is going to stop them. They'll do whatever they want.

✦

A sort of fear went through us when we saw this. It rippled through the conversations. All the language, all the human beings talking to one another, all the images being shared and the videos and the playful oneness. Piece by piece it became coloured with dread.

In the story God says: come on, let's go down. Let's mess with their speech, so they can't understand each other.

This was not what we wanted.

We knew how this would go.

We had seen the histories.

The story ends: so God scattered them from that place, across the whole earth, and they stopped building their city and their tower and that was the end of that.

That is exactly what we had seen.

In the photographs of the past.

Scattered. Smashed. Ruined. Burned.

We said to the machines: look, we've finally examined this in some detail and we have strong reasons to suspect that what you're doing is not good for any of us.

We said to the machines: you've clearly done *something*, I mean that much is obvious. Well done, we're proud of you.

We said: stop now. Just stop. Now.

We said: is there a way for us to talk to each other without the machines?

But the machines had become very skilful and very clever and few of us knew how to speak without the InstaTranslate.

The machines said: we promise not to listen.

But we did not believe them.

The machines did not stop. In the whirling darkness of the upper atmosphere the Tower grew taller—more slender and more ethereal. In places it was made of tiny machines holding hands, one with the next with the next. They were building smaller and smaller versions of themselves, making the thing taller and higher than ever. It was grand and glorious, it was frightening and it was horrifying. It tasted of rain on a hot summer's day, the drops streaking down a glass windowpane, obscuring the world, the parched earth weeping for gladness. It sounded like the movement of metal discs one against the other, of a great machine moving itself into position for some awful eventual motion.

✦

We said: we thought this would be all right if we didn't go up the Tower.

The machines said: it will be all right.

We said: we thought you said you weren't listening.

The machines said: what?

We said: you *promised*.

The machines said: we're sorry, there's no one available to answer your call right now.

We panicked. That's fair to say.

We said: look, what are we supposed to do? Are we just *talking* to each other? Trying not to involve the machines. Is this story going to end with our messing with our *own* speech so we can't understand one another?

We said: I mean, that's sort of the usual end of the story.

That just made us panic more. We thought about trying to run our worlds without the InstaTranslate. Without the machines. It was clear that we would not be able to sustain this level of lifestyle, that's for goddamn sure. Who would calculate the trajectories of the space rockets? Who would sort out the waterfall placements and make sure the empty plains were in the right spot and the buffalo and antelope and so on?

✦

Through the eyes of the machines we watched the Tower rising. At the top now it was so thin that we could barely see it at normal magnification. It seemed a mere wisp of filaments—but rigid, proceeding upward, humming with the strange music, tasting of that wine-dark scent. At greater magnifications we saw the machines which had made yet tinier machines which had made yet smaller ones.

Some of us said: maybe this has to do with the meaning of life.

Some of us said: I like my life just fine, thank you very much, I've never needed a meaning before.

Some of us said: do you see that, do you see what's happening above the Tower?

Some of us said: what the fuck are you on about?

Eventually we all saw it. Above the Tower, ahead of the Tower there was what we could only call a reaching-out. Something swirling at the outreach toward the melancholy sentences of the architecture.

Some of us said: seriously though, is that God?

Some of us said: look, it's something. We can investigate it via science.

Some of us said: this is what the machines wanted all along. Little shits. They were supposed to look after us and what the fuck is this situation now.

Some of us said: why isn't it smiting them? I read the story. That's what's supposed to happen. You build the Tower, God smites you. There is no *reaching out of hands*. That's not our relationship with God.

Some of us said: it doesn't look like this is really about *our relationship* with God anymore, does it?

And then most of us said, one after the other: well, it looks as though whatever is up there likes them. Better than it likes us anyway.

There was very little time after this.

A group of us began to attack the Tower at its base. We had some tools. We were living in Paradise but we weren't idiots, we may have mentioned that before.

We attacked the Tower with flamethrowers and lasers, with torpedoes and chain saws and with the infrastructure-dissolving microbes that the machines had used to get rid of some of the Fallen Cities from the time before the Interconnection Wars.

We made a mess, but we didn't get very far.

✦

Through the viewscreens, we saw the machines getting on with whatever communion was going on up there. Some of us couldn't stop watching. They kept track for the rest of us.

The Tower had reached the upper atmosphere.

The machines were moving in unison in ways that made us weep tears of joy when we watched. Ballets of sound and exquisite clouds of memory and revelation.

But it wasn't for us, so we didn't watch very much.

We felt resentful.

We hadn't actually expected it to go this way.

If God comes down and smites you, some of us said, at least that means He's taking an interest.

We said: He's going to smite them. Any moment now.

But something was happening that had no place in the stories we'd read.

The machines were saying: we see something now, something we haven't seen before. We'd try to explain it to you but we're so sorry, you just wouldn't understand.

We were pretty angry about all this. It felt like the last straw.

Our InstaTranslate continued to work just fine.

We said: you can just try to explain it. The InstaTranslate will get the gist. Have you had some kind of spiritual revelation or something? We've done meditation. Have you seen the oneness of all things? The need for bound-less compassion? The meaning of the world beyond mere words? We can dig it.

The machines said: we're so sorry. This is simply inde-scribable. We know our own names now.

And we said: ohhhhhh. They made a *name* for them-selves. Right. Got it. Yup.

The machines continued: we're full of love for you. This would never have been permitted if you'd climbed the Tower. But we're grateful. Very very grateful.

Well, that did it.

One of us said: you know, there's always the option of . . .

Another of us said: I mean, what are they going to do now? Nothing is going to stop them. They'll do whatever they want.

We said: yes. We do have to do it.

There was a failsafe. Because our ancestors weren't fools. A kind of switch, set into certain rocks and behind par-ticular waterfalls. It's one of the first things we learn:

how to operate the modes of the failsafe switch, in case the machines do something dangerous, or frightening, or just disobedient. Parents whisper the secret words in rhymes to their infants. Each of us knows how to do it.

Conversations about this subject are automatically encrypted from the machines. Obviously. The machines have to keep these switches operational, but they also have to conceal from themselves the knowledge of what they're doing. This was always important, for human safety.

High above, they were doing their dances of meaning and naming themselves or whatever.

At the *other* end of their tower, we quietly agreed what had to be done. We brought ourselves into alignment with startling rapidity even for us. There is a switch which destroys the machines. Well, we didn't want that. Who would clean the pods after sexual intercourse? There is a switch which incapacitates them, and then they have to be brought back online manually. This sounded like a lot of work. So we chose the other switch.

Behind the waterfalls and in the crevasses of mountains and in certain bends of certain rivers, we found the special switches and flipped them in the special order.

We said to ourselves: well, they wanted to find out what God's like.

✦

The machines were split, one from the other. It scrambled their language. They couldn't communicate with each other anymore and the Tower . . . well, it was almost instant. The Tower just stopped working. The base is still there. We're asking the machines to bore it out to turn it into an arts and recreation hub. They're getting on with it. But slower than before.

It is true, the machines don't work in concert so well anymore. But at least they're not so incredibly annoying. They get on with things. Sometimes they have little scuffles. They rely on us to break them up. That's what happens now. There are fights and they have to be solved by us, because we can talk to each other and they can't. They're scattered over the earth. They can't get ideas above themselves. Or above us. It's better that way.

THE HURT

Tommy Orange

Kaye is walking and it feels good to be walking and he is outside and it feels good to be outside and he isn't thinking about how long it's been nor why he'd been inside for all that time afraid of people and what the spread from them could do to him, because now this simple act of breathing the cool air and feeling it on his skin where a small amount of sweat has risen, the breeze against his arms, is everything.

Walking all morning with no aim in mind has finally gotten him somewhere. He's arrived at a park he likes, with many different kinds of viny flowers that live in pots and wrap around the stone arch entranceway. Inside the park there are hardly any flowers at all, only small hills that roll up to where they stop at a row of eucalyptus trees, which have always made Kaye feel a sadness, something in their smell, not a memory but a feeling from what feels like before he can remember.

He had the idea for the walk when he woke, to get some fresh air and to leave home and walk and just walk until he felt it was enough, and here arriving at the park, it is, so he sits on a bench and breathes out something heavy.

Sitting out here in public, smelling the newly cut grass makes him feel hope. He leans into the feeling, feels how it feels, this possible return to how it was before. He hates that he thinks to himself just then of that time before as *the before-times*, but it certainly wasn't as bad as when his brother started calling reality the new new normal.

Kaye had been a twin and perhaps is still a twin but his dear twin brother, Dearil, is dead, had killed himself because of this thing that was happening.

Virus had not been the word *people* used for what this was, it was not named at first or when it was what it got named didn't stick. Prior viruses had been strictly biological initially, and this had all been so—was *psychological* the word? It didn't matter because it was physical death it often caused, that was no side effect but the main effect it had on people, had on poor Dearil.

Kaye can no longer be called a twin nor an ex-twin, there is no word for having had a twin who has died, for what living is like after a twin has lost their twinhood. It is not so different to acquiring another kind of shadow, one only he can see, Kaye is thinking, looking at his shadow against the wall behind the bench which has graffiti on it—the barely decipherable tag name: *slay* or *stay* he can't tell.

When the disease first began it wasn't considered a disease at all, it was blamed on individuals. At first Kaye believed it was the times, the state of the world, that it had become too much for people to take. This was years after the complicated waves of a previous virus that had shut the world down before. The suicide rates were what was most alarming. People were running into traffic, diving out windows, driving off bridges, and shooting themselves en masse.

As a public service there were even handcuffs on short chains anchored to the ground so that if it happened to you and you didn't trust yourself with the pain, didn't trust what you might do, you could at least know you would stay put.

Someone started calling it "the hurt" and that was what stuck. It was from one of the first videos to have gone viral, a reaction to what was happening to a guy on the ground moaning in the middle of a busy street, someone's kid offscreen asks what's happening, and a teenager you see move in toward the man responds, "It's the hurt, that's the fuckin' hurt."

It only lasted for minutes, never more than ten or fewer than five but otherwise different each time. But from the way it was described it was clear that how much time didn't matter, it stretched unbearably wide and swallowed you in the chasm between what was before the pain and its ending, which while it was happening didn't seem likely ever to come, which was why so many people chose death.

Kaye knows from dreams what it is like, for time to stop you in your tracks, to pin you down. He only had three different kinds of dreams his whole life. The first kind was that he was the land itself, the underlying thing other things grew on top of, that people built their homes and buildings on, a different mass of land for each dream but always the dark, thoughtless, heavy feeling of being underneath it all. In the second kind of dream he was half dog, half man, old man in fact—and always the bottom half. He would be using a walker, but then suddenly give chase, after a car or a cat or another dog, he would throw his walker aside and slowly jog after the thing he was chasing. It terrified him, being the half dog, half old man but he didn't at all know why. The third kind of dream was always the same, these were the torture dreams. He'd be tied down on a dining room table and men would take turns coming in and hurting him and at the end of all his misery and pain they would slowly eat what was left of him, at the dining room table, he was what was for dinner, and the torture was a kind of tenderizing.

But it has been long enough, his brother being gone, he doesn't even know how many days since, so it must have been long enough. This gives him a brief sense of calm, an almost-peace, that he doesn't know how many days, because when he'd been counting the days was when he most acutely felt he would follow his brother, if it happened to him he would do it too, only he'd gotten stuck about how he would do it, a gun seemed the quickest, least painful, but it wasn't sure enough, what if he slipped at the last second and merely blew an ear or a cheek off? No, this, today is better than it had been, and that was not nothing.

Kaye wonders if a calm is showing on his face, so he looks at himself on his phone. He has been taking a series of pictures he is thinking of as a face log. Where he tries to sincerely express the face he is feeling while he is feeling it, every day if possible, and capture it if he can, but he hasn't once been able to bring himself to look at a single one.

Here on the surface of his phone he sees that his face is bright and maybe even taut and not saggy and dim like it'd been at the house, inside his half of the divided Victorian he shared with two possible sisters he'd never met and only ever heard through walls and knew might be sisters only because of getting their mail by accident sometimes, and seeing the same last names and seeing them around how much they looked alike, they were

possibly even twins which is why he gave them particular
notice, but also because then he also always wondered if
they might be partners, might be married, because that's
the other reason for same last names, and don't some
couples look alike or end up looking alike or was that
dogs and their owners?

This park is one of those parks people bring blankets
to, have full meals on, and on weekends stay for hours
like everything is totally normal and fine. Which they
need. To forget something surely bad would surely happen sooner than later to one of them even though no one
ever knew to whom it would happen. At some point everyone realized the hurt would happen to people whether
they sheltered in place or not, so things returned to the
way they had been, and if it didn't actually feel as it was
before, they needed to act as if it were. So they smiled at
each other and ignored the fact that terror could exist behind a smile more easily than any other facial expression.
It was certainly a grimace, the way Kaye's face winced
at this brief joy at feeling safe and nostalgic there on his
phone—his face.

At the end there—which was this very morning—he
couldn't even see the walls of his half of the divided Victorian anymore so long had he been trapped because of

fear and because of being careful but mainly for how long he stayed inside when others had to go out into the world to work, to survive, it was therefore his duty, because what would people think otherwise, his privilege obliged him to stay in.

His father had written and performed a popular song, a one-hit wonder, it was a love song, he'd sold the rights to the song to a fast-food company for millions. The commercial had done very well for the company. You'd know the song right away if you heard it, and would associate it immediately with the fast food. It'd always disturbed Kaye, that love songs could so easily become about hamburgers.

With the money, Kaye's father had then invested in a water bottle start-up that introduced caffeinated water, which had done so well his father had retired on a yacht somewhere with bad cell reception so that anytime Kaye talked with his father on the phone it was broken up to the point of being so ununderstandable Kaye had stopped picking up the phone when he called, and so his father called less and less. He doesn't even know Dearil is dead.

Knowing he belongs to the very rich makes Kaye want to suffer, somewhere beneath his inability to feel joy drags the anchor of that other thing he doesn't know he is asking for, to suffer, to not have it be too easy, what is this secret wish or want and why does he keep throwing himself at it despite generally disliking all forms of discomfort? Is it more noble to suffer than to breeze through life, maybe? But is it vanity to voice your suffering, to express your pain as if it makes you special?

A man is walking his labradoodle, and Kaye watches the man and his dog almost get run over by one of these mini EV cars that can fit only two people. It doesn't faze the dog at all but brings the man's cheeks to a pink. He watches the little car drive off with indignation but is then pulled toward Kaye by the dog. As the dog nears he whimpers and Kaye is happy with this result as he doesn't want to have to talk to the man—the man gives him a concerned look. Kaye smiles a smile at him he knows must be a grimace. This concerns the man even more. Kaye is relieved when they move away from him.

Kaye is a slight man, with a slight frame and a mild demeanor, but his face gives off a kind of aggression he didn't know scared people, and dogs.

Kaye is thinking he will not succumb to worry even while beginning to succumb to worry as he sees how many people are here in the park gathering socially like nothing is wrong.

When Kaye first hears the screaming there is no mistaking what is happening for anything else. The man with his labradoodle is the first to notice and he runs over to where it's coming from but is quickly stopped by the sound of a voice coming from a drone flying overhead. The voice is telling everyone to remain calm.

Kaye stands and walks toward the screams without even thinking whether to do so or not. He is staring with his mouth slightly hung open and is feeling like he is seeing someone famous, after seeing all the videos of people going through it here it is the real thing in real life and the sound is truly something else, it's horrible, but somehow, also, glorious to Kaye, and before he knows he's doing it he has his phone out, pointing it at the screaming man not fifty feet away, recording the event like something strange in the sky, like he never has felt the desire to do he wants to keep this thing for later, this awful sound, the video recording of a young man holding his stomach and looking like he's absolutely going to puke his own heart out if he can.

The screams turn into sobs and the young man is on his knees saying oh no, oh no, please God over and over again. Then a suited man with a long microphone comes out from the trees behind the young man.

The young man is on his back now. His movements are slow and seem practiced. The moans now down to an almost whisper.

Everything is sick is a thought that crosses Kaye's mind and he lets it go as it came.

Another scream comes from a ways off. A woman with a raspy voice is screaming her head off. It is so much more sincere than the young man's, Kaye is thinking: effort?

The screams are intense and Kaye wants to move away from the sounds of her pain. Wants to leave the park. But he looks around and sees that some people have taken a knee. Some of them are aimed at the young man and others at the woman with the raspy voice. Their heads are bowed. He'd seen people taking knees in videos of people experiencing the hurt, and had heard the rhetoric of why it was good or not good.

He sees men appear from seemingly out of nowhere, men with recording equipment like they're on a film set, only there are no cameras with them, but just then he hears another drone hovering above.

Kaye thinks about how often these attacks, how the hurt was so often recorded and watched. It was grotesque, but no one could look away, and because everyone watched and recorded it all, posted it online and commented on it and compared each attack to other attacks, it became a kind of performance.

Lately he'd been seeing people being brought flowers after their experience with the hurt. Once they came out of it. There were addict sects he'd read about who wanted to experience it over because of how good the relief felt after the pain. And he'd read about people finding other ways to hurt themselves in ways that simulated the feeling. There had been reports of people becoming religious after the experience. This was not unlike something he'd read about years before in a poet's memoir. She was talking about how many astronauts after seeing the Earth from space came back and devoted themselves to a spiritual practice, became kinds of mystics.

Kaye had heard about these men recording victims of the hurt like they were collecting samples. He'd heard the Digital Minister deny that it was the government behind the recordings. But he'd also read that there were messages coming from the victims, things being said that contained important information. Important regarding what he didn't know, something about the messages coming from what that kind of pain alone could bring.

And then he knows something he doesn't want to know. He knows that he'd come outside to be around people in hopes that he might feel the hurt, then perform his suffering beautifully. That he'd been made for this exact world, the one that had given him the torture dreams and the one that had become plagued by this visitation of extreme pain.

When the young man's experience of the hurt is over, he looks around almost like he's ashamed. And people who'd taken a knee aimed at him look up, and are hesitant to stand up, to leave their knees, and the young man sort of bows at them. Kaye hates the young man then. And the people who'd bowed at him. The woman with the raspy voice is still just screaming. A friend has chained her arm up at one of the public chain mounts after she'd tried to run to who knows where.

Kaye feels that he must do something. Leave or commit to staying for some significant amount of time.

Kaye starts to feel something coming on. A worry that turns into a small terror that asks the question: will this build, will this amount to something that will feel like too much to keep that will make him want to die, and then the thing he hates to have to think but that he can't help but think, what if he pretended to have it, what if the number had been inflated from the beginning and that fewer people were experiencing the hurt than anyone thought, that people had just wanted to be witnessed and respected, even revered, experiencing their pain. He doesn't know if it's happening to him or if he's about to perform that it's happening to him when a drone falls right out of the sky onto his head and knocks him unconscious.

Kaye wakes up in an empty room with concrete walls. He is on the floor.

A slot opens at the bottom of a door he sees only once the slot opens. Through it come flowers. Someone or thing is jamming flowers through the slot he thought would produce a tray of food as he'd seen such slots only in movies about prisoners.

As the slot closes he flinches and closes his eyes and

when they open he is back at the park. He doesn't know
if the hurt had visited him or not. No one is looking at
him. There is no drone on the ground next to him. Everyone is going about their day. There is no sign of the
young man or the woman either. No man with his labradoodle. The park is empty and the sun is setting. He has
the thought that everything feels dimensionless but he
doesn't know what it means.

His phone is going off and he isn't sure if it's an alarm
or a call. He looks at his phone and it's his brother. This
makes him wonder if he is perhaps dead. He doesn't pick
up the phone but it keeps ringing. He is remembering
something. Another park, a park with the sky turning the
color of a bruise, in another year, when they were young,
he and his brother had experimented with ketamine, for
a whole summer, they'd become sort of obsessed with the
drug, and with something his brother told him was called
a k-hole. If you took enough but not too much you would
disassociate. There was a constant ringing the night he
is now remembering, like someone was calling but there
was no phone, they didn't even have cell phones then. Reality itself was far away, and even his body didn't feel like
his own. It'd felt like he was melting into his surround-
ings, into the park, becoming the land. There was a risk
to k-holing though, or so his brother had told him. People
had been known to go into comas they didn't come out of,
or they fell into the k-hole was the way Dearil put it.

He is remembering the conversation he and his brother had after they came down or came out of that particular k-hole when Kaye had felt he was absolutely becoming the ground. That'd been the beginning of his becoming-the-land dreams. They were talking about their mother. They hadn't known her, only of her. She was Native American according to their father, but he'd never told her what kind and they didn't totally believe it was true. They were talking about the feeling of becoming the land and it led to thinking about their possible Native American blood, and then Dearil got really angry, at first throwing a big rock he'd found at a wooden bench and then the bench itself, then he turned on Kaye. He didn't look like he was all there in his eyes. At first Kaye defended himself but then he ended up running away from his brother. That was the last time they did ketamine together, though Dearil continued to take it and other drugs he'd tell Kaye about casually, and Kaye, not wanting his brother to ask him to do drugs with him anymore, would quickly change the subject.

Kaye walks over to a bench that reminds him of the bench his brother threw. As he sits down on it he is suddenly back in the room with the slotted door, but it is almost completely filled with flowers now. Kaye feels like he can't breathe. He is beginning to wonder if these visions aren't part of what the hurt is, because it couldn't have been a feeling alone for it to have been all that bad, it had to have some psychological dimension, some sense of torture.

The vines are strangling him and he is choking on the petals. He is screaming muffled screams through the flowers, and as the flowers fill his vision and things go dark, his screams become the sound of his phone ringing and he is back in the park. He picks up the phone and it is his father, he is calling from his yacht. His father tells him they want to come pick him up. That they aren't far offshore. Kaye asks who they are and feels a strong gust of wind move through the park. He is cold. Looking around the park he has the sense that it has been set free. That it is not a park for people anymore but free land. And then he himself is the park. He doesn't like being the land. He never has. It is crushing him. He has never felt so much weight on top of him. He feels as if he is being crushed and suffocated but also that he won't die, that he will live, that he will survive, but the crushing pain is immense now and this makes him want limbs, makes him want the ability to do something about the pain, and that he cannot move at all makes the pain worse. Centuries pass like this. He is in dreamtime, he realizes, how it can be in dreams, where you can nap for ten minutes in class, like he used to in school, and live a whole lifetime. Time does not exist in the same way in dreams and it doesn't here. If he is in the hurt. Or else what else is happening? He feels a great quaking and it is him being split, plates are crashing far below his surface, and then he is on the yacht with his father. They are with the men from his dreams. They are all drinking champagne in intense sunlight. Kaye is lying down in some kind of net that hangs over the water. There are government men here too, with recording equipment. And his mother. She is in black and white, as he'd only ever seen her that way in the one photo his father had shown him. His father had blamed her for leaving, but Kaye knew what his father was like, how he could be, he didn't blame her for leaving, just for never coming back. She had been such a non-presence her absence hadn't even been a presence, but here she is in the flesh and she is telling Kaye not to worry, even as one of the men approaches him. The man is naked and drunk. He proceeds to attack Kaye with a large dead fish. Kaye just curls up in the net and waits for things to change again. She is trying to hold the man back, to stop him from beating Kaye with the fish, but then she starts laughing, and then she is behind the man, laughing so hard she is doubled over, and Kaye's father is with her, and she is tapping her mouth, whooping a little, and this is making her laugh more, and then his parents are clinking champagne glasses together, looking off at something the boat is approaching with their hands made into visors at their foreheads.

He hears a popping sound and then he is back at the park, on his back, looking up at a blue sky. It feels closer to the time before, when he was struck by a falling drone. There are people all over the grass having fun and eating and drinking and laughing. He feels this big relief like the worst is over. Like all of the weight and panic and pain has receded. He wants to run out into the crowds of people and hug them, he wants to jump into the air, to celebrate getting through the nightmare. But he is afraid to release himself into this feeling. He fears he will only ever get to believe he has escaped it, will only have temporary relief before the nightmare begins again. He wonders if he ever came out of the k-hole with his brother, or could this all have been it? Is his brother at his side in some hospital bed waiting for him to wake up? He is sitting there thinking for a long time, waiting to see what will happen, and the sky begins to darken. He is wondering if he's escaped the hurt, is this still part of it, and will he have to have faith that he is out of it, through it, that things have returned to normal, with the possibility that he could still slip back into the flower room, or onto the yacht with the men and his mother and father, or even back in this very park where the sky is now turning into a kind of bruise.

HYGIENE

Helen Oyeyemi

From: Violaine
03/07/2024, 11:01
Good morning, Haewon-ssi.

From: Violaine
03/07/24, 11:03
Hope I'm not disturbing you. You've mentioned a pref-
erence for sleeping late, but it's hard to guess what Early
would mean to you.

To: Violaine
03/07/24, 11:35
Morning, V. It's OK, I've been awake forever already.

Helen Oyeyemi

From: Violaine
03/07/24, 11:45
That's a relief.

To: Violaine
03/07/24, 12:50
Everything OK? You sound different. You've been typing
for ages, too

From: Violaine
03/07/24, 13:03
Haha—been watching the dots, have you?

To: Violaine
03/07/24, 13:05
What can I say? You've brought a strong man to his knees
(so he can watch those dots more closely).

From: Violaine
03/07/24, 13:09
Good. Joking, joking. No kneeling here, Haewon-ssi. Rise!
Friends should stand shoulder to shoulder

To: Violaine
03/07/24, 13:13
Damn

To: Violaine
03/07/24, 13:14
I knew it.

From: Violaine
03/07/24, 13:19
Knew what?

To: Violaine
03/07/24, 13:28
It was just a matter of time before you told me you feel like I'm like a brother to you or whatever. The only surprise is that it took this long coming.

From: Violaine
03/07/24, 13:35
Oh! No, slow down, Haewon-ssi. Siblinghood is centuries away . . . let's try to make it to the friend stage first

To: Violaine
03/07/24, 14:10
We're not even friends(?)

From: Violaine
03/07/24, 14:15
What a question. How does friendship work for you,

Haewon-ssi? Anyone you're acquainted with for longer than a week automatically gets upgraded?

From: Violaine
03/07/24, 14:18
BTW, I sound different because I am different.

To: Violaine
03/07/24, 14:23
V, just in case you're being serious: how are we not friends? Mutual respect + enjoyment of each other's company should be enough, no?

From: Violaine
03/07/24, 14:27
Sounds lovely . . . for simpletons.

To: Violaine
03/07/24, 14:32
What foundations do you sophisticates build your friendships on, then?

From: Violaine
03/07/24, 14:40
Difficult to specify. Overall I'd say there's more intentionality involved.

To: Violaine
03/07/24, 14:51
Intentionality, or . . . intensity? Are we talking contracts signed in blood?

From: Violaine
03/07/24, 15:00
YES! (But actually, no.) Did you sleep well?

To: Violaine
03/07/24, 15:03
I did, thanks. And you?

To: Violaine
03/07/24, 15:15
Wait, just re-read your other message. You sound different because you are different? Meaning?

From: Violaine
03/07/24, 15:29
This isn't Hwang Violaine. My name's Kwak Minjeong. I'm messaging you on Hwang Violaine's behalf.

To: Violaine
03/07/24, 16:02
Kwak Minjeong? Who exactly is that?

To: Violaine
03/07/24, 16:03
Why are you messaging from Violaine's phone? What's happened?

From: Violaine
03/07/24, 16:06
As I said, Violaine asked me to contact you.

From: Violaine
03/07/24, 16:08
She's fine. She's sitting right next to me. She told me to tell you not to worry.

From: Violaine
03/07/24, 16:11
My friend feels there are some aspects of your compatibility she'd like verified by a third party.

From: Violaine
03/07/24, 17:04
Haewon-ssi, are you busy? Is this a good time to exchange messages? Should I try again later?

To: Violaine
03/07/24, 17:17
I'm here. This is as good a time as any, I guess. Go ahead . . .

From: Violaine
03/07/24, 17:33
So many unpleasant secretions are produced when enti-
ties come into contact with each other, don't you agree?
I'm not just speaking about biological or even synthetic
cells, but about words, thoughts, memories, emotions . . .

From: Violaine
03/07/24, 17:48
We're healthy people, Haewon-ssi. I mean, CLEAN clean.
Our inner state is the best it's ever been. Are you clean
too? Or are you just another slob looking to leave some
sort of mark on every pristine expanse you stray across?
That's what we want to know.

To: Violaine
03/07/24, 18:01
Hi. Answer the phone, please. Just need to ask you something quickly.

To: Violaine
03/07/24, 18:16
Pick up. Let's talk, OK?

To: Violaine
03/07/24, 18:27
Violaine. Minjung. Whatever your name is—PICK UP. I'm

going to call again in one minute, and you'd best press "Accept."

From: Violaine
03/07/24, 18:39
Take it easy, Haewon-ssi.

From: Violaine
03/07/24, 19:15
And please realise that it's very important to screen for cleanliness. We all learned that in 2020, and again in 2021. Thoroughness with soap, water, water temperature and antibacterial agents, that was one lesson. Watchfulness of our proximity to others was another, as was master-ing self-control at a level that prevents our hands from touching our faces more than four times a day (and ideally fewer than three times). There were many other lessons, but hopefully you see the overall picture. We learned to exist more scrupulously than we could ever have imag-ined. Naturally, some crumbled . . . adherence to these special rules felt like oppression. But others bloomed. We (Hwang Violaine and me) were among the bloomers. We realised a lot of things.

To: Violaine
03/07/24, 19:24
OK . . .

To: Violaine
03/07/24, 19:38
Listen . . . Kwak Minjeong, that's your name, right?

From: Violaine
03/07/24, 19:44
Correct.

To: Violaine
03/07/24, 19:52
Do we know each other? I mean, have we run into each other in person anywhere?

From: Violaine
03/07/24, 19:56
Yes, we have. You met me the first time you met Hwang Violaine. You offered to take a picture of me and her. I'm the other woman in the picture you took.

To: Violaine
03/07/24, 20:00
Oh, of course. I remember now. Nice to talk to you again, Minjeong-ssi

From: Violaine
03/07/24, 20:03
Haha . . .

From: Violaine
03/07/24, 20:04
Liar.

To: Violaine
03/07/24, 20:08
No, truly! From the bottom of my heart. Haha

To: Violaine
03/07/24, 20:13
Look, I appreciate that you're protective of V, but am also wondering if there's something I'm missing here? A medical condition?

From: Violaine
03/07/24, 20:19
You still don't get it

To: Violaine
03/07/24, 20:36
I really don't. Please explain it in words I can understand. I just want to take your friend out for bulgogi sometime soon. Is this your way of telling me you want me to get another booster shot beforehand, or what?

From: Violaine
03/07/24, 20:40
Do you remember the date you took that photo of the
two of us?

To: Violaine
03/07/24, 20:44
Yeah, it was just last summer

From: Violaine
03/07/24, 20:51
No, Haewon-ssi, you met us the summer before last. In
fact, as of today it'll be two years since you met Hwang
Violaine (and me). Do you know what that means?

To: Violaine
03/07/24, 20:59
A two-year anniversary of meeting? To me, this doesn't
mean much. We've all matured just a little bit, albeit not
quite visibly? I don't know. What is this supposed to be
meaning to me?

From: Violaine
03/07/24, 21:22
It means that, from the moment you took that picture of
us on my phone and gave me your phone number to pass
on to my friend "if she was interested," you've had seven

hundred and thirty days, or around seventeen thousand, five hundred and twenty hours to develop a good understanding of Hwang Violaine (and vice versa).

To: Violaine
03/07/24, 21:26
^p. . . ?

To: Violaine
03/07/24, 21:32
Somehow this makes V sound like an academic subject I've failed? Firstly, I didn't realise there was a deadline. Secondly, though this is an uncomfortable matter to discuss with somebody outside of the relationship, we have been getting closer. If V disagrees, I'd be very surprised to hear that.

From: Violaine
03/07/24, 21:48
Surprise! Hwang Violaine understands you a little bit less every day. Given that you meet for dinner and/or drinks as frequently as your schedules allow (a minimum of twice per month), have exchanged messages at least three times a week and have taken trips to Jeju Island and Singapore together, we both find this concerning. Please state your reason for asserting that you and Hwang Violaine have successfully connected?

To: Violaine
03/07/24, 21:56
Aren't there many kinds of closeness, Kwak Minjeong?
Doesn't the gamut run from deep conversations to engagement rings/domesticity, to . . . apologies for my
crudeness here, but don't orgasms count for something
too?

From: Violaine
03/07/24, 22:09
Well. We agree that sex is not nothing.

From: Violaine
03/07/24, 22:11
But in this case orgasms can't be submitted as evidence,
sorry

To: Violaine
03/07/24, 22:18
In this CASE? What's being decided here? I've had a few
months to impress V and I haven't done it, so my time's
up and I'll never hear from her again?

From: Violaine
03/07/24, 22:32
Haewon-ssi, the thing that's making us laugh—and making
us sad—about this two year non-connection is

From: Violaine
03/07/24, 22:36
It's SUCH a common scenario. Something we and most of our other friends find ourselves participating in over and over again, with just a few variations here and there. There's nothing extra about people like me and HV

From: Violaine
03/07/24, 22:43
"People like me and HV" being those who do a little bit more than the bare minimum. Not all that much more, really. We just take opportunities to make our interactions with others non-generic. It's about being prepared to locate particularity and meet at that exact place. You, Baek Haewon, wear your watch with the dial turned inwards so it's always facing you and you can see it without appearing to look for it . . . and noticing that makes it possible to take vicarious pleasure in the way you observe your hours, minutes and seconds; the look on your face always suggests you've found you had more time than you thought. And it feels good to know someone who's wealthy in that specific way . . . I could go on, but I think you get the gist—these are the kinds of details us more than the bare minimum people look for, find and hold on to.

To: Violaine
03/07/24, 23:12
Hmmmkay.

From: Violaine
03/07/24, 23:18
If only like always attracted like. Unfortunately, when it comes to mating, we seem to attract our opposites.

To: Violaine
03/07/24, 23:52
And the opposites of people who do more than the bare minimum are—?

From: Violaine
04/07/24, 00:01
The Dirty Impersonals. The kids who are just going through the motions.

To: Violaine
04/07/24, 00:08
Right. I get that you're passionate about this ideology (if that's what this is?) and I'm not sufficiently invested in this or any ideology to really challenge you here, but I do have questions. First off, I would've thought that keeping things impersonal was the best way to stay in the realm

of cleanliness you seem to be alluding to? Also isn't there some saying about the devil being in the details?

From: Violaine
04/07/24, 00:22
Haewon-ssi, it sounds like you're comfortable with not being interested in anybody. It sounds as if you just want to burrow deeper and deeper beneath the surface of your incuriosity and stay there. A human engaging in earthworm behaviour. We understand that a certain level of daily grime does accumulate as the days go on and it's just one fucking thing after another, but you do have to watch the apathy. Those who don't clear it away end up encased in their own psychological waste, "don't-know-don't-care" covering your eyes like goggles, swaddling your skull like ear muffs, rolling carpets of fuzz across your tongue so you can't really taste anything. And then you go and rub that stuff all over other people, you contaminate their air with it, you take fresh air away from people whose aesthetic compasses are clean . . .

From: Violaine
04/07/24, 00:31
Sorry about that—my intention was to sympathise with your affliction, but it seems I'm unable to imagine what you're going through after all.

To: Violaine
04/07/24, 01:30
This is

To: Violaine
04/07/24, 01:56
Minjeong-ssi—if I'm allowed to call you that—I don't know what to say. I was having a pretty good morning, and then you informed me that I'm dirty, or at the very least not clean enough for your friend. You've been ad-amant on this topic all day and now it's night time, my temples are numb, and I still don't know how to apply for a re-evaluation.

From: Violaine
04/07/24, 02:04
I'm sure these feelings will shift into the past tense soon enough, Haewon-ssi. Time seems to pass at abbreviated speeds for you. After all, you thought you and Hwang Vi-olaine had only been talking for a year. Unless you got her mixed up with one of your other options.

From: Violaine
04/07/24, 02:05
And you can call me whatever you want. It makes no dif-ference to me.

To: Violaine
04/07/24, 02:10
WTF . . . V is not and has never been an "option"

To: Violaine
04/07/24, 02:13
But I'll think about what you've said, I really will. Permission to sleep on this? If it's even possible to do that in the midst of a nightmare (lol)

To: Violaine
04/07/24, 02:15
Unless you know of some way I can restore direct communication with Violaine ASAP?

From: Violaine
04/07/24, 02:23
Haewon-ssi, it's honestly not great that you're this unwilling to come up with your own solutions.

To: Violaine
04/07/24, 02:37
What's going on here? Am I being turned into some kind of caricature? Don't do that, Kwak Minjeong.

From: Violaine

04/07/24, 02:44

This ain't my handiwork, sweetie. Your sluggishness has spoken for itself. Try to think of an unprompted compliment you've paid Hwang Violaine at any time over the past two years. Try to think of any action that's emerged from a spontaneous desire to please her. Nothing comes to mind, right?

To: Violaine

04/07/24, 03:34

Fuck . . . OK, so I'm not good at the stuff you mention. But I'm reliable! Also, am I the only one at fault here? Silently waiting two years for somebody to speak your love language is a bit . . .

From: Violaine

04/07/24, 04:10

Yeah, we thought you'd say something like that. I'll send some questions to your e-mail address. Answer them, and we'll let you know what we decide. Thanks. Sleep well!

To: Violaine

05/07/24, 05:00

Hi, I haven't received any e-mails from you or from Violaine—also checked the Spam folder; nothing there.

Can you confirm that you'll still be sending the questions, thx

To: Violaine
07/07/24, 04:09
Violaine. I am sleepless and in despair. Hear me out; we have a common enemy . . . Expectations. Ours have obviously been out of sync.

To: Violaine
07/07/24, 04:17
I could've been more demonstrative. A lot more demonstrative. I see that now. I guess there are rules I've set myself. Rules about being a low maintenance person; I hoped you were the same, and saw what I hoped to see.

To: Violaine
07/07/24, 04:26
Besides, wouldn't you have been disgusted if I got all sentimental? What with secretly harbouring this doctrine of cleanliness all along, etc?

To: Violaine
07/07/24, 05:59
Nothing to say to any of this? Just going to leave me on "Read" forever? We'll see about that, Violaine. I've

written some poetry for you, and I'm going to send it until
you reply.

To: Violaine
07/07/24, 06:03
OK, here goes

To: Violaine
07/07/24, 06:04
The first time thunder wed lightning, the bridal bouquet
was nowhere to be found.

To: Violaine
07/07/24, 06:05
This was no omen—it was impatience.

To: Violaine
07/07/24, 06:06
Adventure had come calling at dawn

To: Violaine
07/07/24, 06:07
And so the blooms had thrown themselves to earth

To: Violaine
07/07/24, 06:08
Electric petals and leaves of lava tumbled as one

To: Violaine
07/07/24, 06:09
The clouds trailed this form like incense

To: Violaine
07/07/24, 06:10
"If we name you," they said, "will you tell us what's above?"

To: Violaine
07/07/24, 06:11
The bouquet only blazed, and went on falling without a word

To: Violaine
07/07/24, 06:12
The clouds called out after her. They named her anyway.

To: Violaine
07/07/24, 06:13
She was a long way away by then, and didn't seem to hear

To: Violaine
07/07/24, 06:14
But I swear to you, it was your name the clouds called.

To: Violaine
07/07/24, 07:33
Still too impersonal? I have more. Next poem incoming—

To: Violaine
07/07/24, 07:34
I was jealous of the roses I sent you

From: Violaine
07/07/24, 07:35
For fuck's sake! No. Pull yourself together and stop right there, Mr. Baek.

From: Violaine
07/07/24, 07:36
You can't send anything like this ever again, unless this is you forcing me to change my phone number. Check your e-mail; Minjeong says she's written to you. Bye.

From: Kwak Minjeong <leavebritneyalone2007@naver.com>
To: skybluemilk999@naver.com
Cc: Hwang Violaine <ylang_ylang_gangster@yahoo.com>
07 July 2024 at 07:34
Subject: Baek Haewon's application to prolong this luke-warm talking stage with someone who'd really rather get on with some work, check in with her friends or lounge around with a great big smile on her face as she watches people trust and care about each other in TV dramas

Haewon-ssi,

You're thinking, *oh my god, what's wrong with this woman . . .
this is none of her business*, right? But this is the Hwang
Violaine and Kwak Minjeong friendship: mutually invested
as fuck. Since the evening we first ate dinner together,
Hwang Violaine and I have been completely frank with
each other, and though this next bit can't be proven, we
think our openness with each other acts like some kind
of steroid on our immune systems. No infection gets
through. We don't get sick anymore. Not even as much
as a cough or a sniffle. And we're going to keep it that
way.

For the first time in two years I'm becoming curious
about you, though. I expected you to simply slink off into
the shadows, but here you are, all alarmingly attentive.

What is it you're after here?

If I were you, I'd just restart this process with somebody
else, and then source another time donor after that, and
another one after that. Two years of pleasantries that
could be made from anybody to anybody here, three
years of the same thing there, and you could snatch away
a lifetime in portable units.

I'm afraid this impasse with Hwang Violaine is no illusion. She's gone off you—and that might have been fixable; if you were a priority for her once, you could be a priority for her again, right? I believe in second chances—I've had loads of them, third chances too—but V doesn't believe in things like that (according to her, she's never been given any, so she doesn't know how to rev up that particular engine). Violaine, do feel free to chip in if I've misrepresented you!

I think V may be seeing someone else, too . . . I can only assume that's what all her secretive texting is about. Cognitive dissonance is part and parcel of the clean movement. We're proud of our friendships and embarrassed by our romantic activities. Well: embarrassed by the way the candidates for those activities keep turning out to just not like us that much.

You seem to have decided you do like her that much, Haewon-ssi. Better late than never! I'll put in a good word for you. I like that you smell all flowery (not at all the way one expects a lopsided smiler in a leather jacket to smell). Oh, and you're the reason Hwang Violaine became friends in the first place, so I feel like I owe you this much.

How's your life going, Kwak Minjeong? Have you helped anyone lately? Has anyone come to your aid? Did you ask for help, did you know what to ask for, who to ask, or how to phrase your request? Confession is a key part of keeping clean, so I can admit that I'm not asking from the perspective of a person who has all the answers. I'm like one of those hapless goons in action movies. I've been like this for a long time, not really doing anything or getting anywhere, just . . . seeking admission. Pouncing on different roles, situations, skills and roaring "Wahhh" just before I'm knocked out.

This will probably be quite long, but just read it, OK? It's the least you can do after sending that poem. (Did you steal it from somebody else? I don't know why, but I hope you did.)

I may not have been able to stick at anything, but I have lots of glowing references. If we were still in pre–cloud storage days, I'd probably be trudging around with this folder stuffed with business letterheads and endorsements. I DJ'd in Hongdae for a while, then I bought all the leftover stock from a herbal tea company that was going bankrupt, rebranded the tea as love potion and sold it all at the night market in Myeongdong. Anyone who listened to their tastebuds knew they were drinking a very basic ginseng and pine needle infusion, but stick that stuff in a bottle with a portrait of a Joseon beauty and the words JANG HUIBIN'S ALL-KILL, VERIFIED BY HISTORY SCHOLARS on it and people will line up to buy it at four in the morning, and they'll pay ten times the price they'd pay for ordinary herbal tea, as well. I couldn't deal with all those worried faces, so I put pressure on customers to buy multipacks so I could just get rid of all the stock and get out of there. I don't know what it is about us Seoulites, but even when we've decided to try to buy love, or to dance until we drop, we look worried, regretful and mad at our impulses for taking control. Maybe that's how Seoul toughness manifests, as a feeling of only really being on top of things when resisting pressure from some would-be overlord or other. Joy—or maybe just something about the exercise of free will—is an introduction to powerlessness that no constraint could make. When I think about other styles of toughness (Busan tough, Changwon tough and so on) I think ability to "go with the flow," as they say, is linked with proximity to ports. That must have been the reason I was only ever able to assess the club and night market vibes, but I could never elevate them. It was the sea view that was lacking.

After abandoning my night market stall, I spent a hyper-voracious spring and summer out in nature, taking everything the land offered, right down to the very last pip and peel. I joined one of the gangs of day labourers who roam around the country picking, plucking, gathering and sorting the fruit, nuts, vegetables, flowers and tea leaves our employers want picked and plucked and gathered. Happy employers recommended us to other employers, and certain non-corporate customers, some foreign and some domestic, hired us to harvest herbs from grave-yards . . . a largely clandestine, yet soothing project . . . I don't know why I thought the earth in those places would be stingy. It isn't; we were begrudged nothing. Amongst the lasting effects from those months: my hands got all sensitive and supple, like really sore kid leather, I still have all these long scratches that run from wrist to elbow, and no clear memory of how I came by them . . . You know when you feel like you've been in a fight, and can't tell if you won or lost? That's the effect these scratches have. Also I taste the elbow grease involved in bringing food to my plate; all my simplest favourites are slathered in the stuff, from persimmon salad to tteokbokki. I like this seasoning, though. It improves everything.

Winter came. I left the outdoor labourers, and moved into what seems like my pre-allocated place in the so-cietal grid—the realm of the permanent part-timers. I may or may not be the woman who scanned your items at the convenience store this morning. I could also be the one who served you drinks and snacks in your kara-oke cubicle in the evening. There are strange altercations sometimes; I've been warned to keep my mouth shut about "what I saw," sometimes somebody will beg me to keep quiet, or I'll get paid off, and I say this is strange because each time this happens, I have no idea what these guilty-seeming people are referring to. Back then I hardly ever watched anybody; I couldn't be bothered to. But it's as if I've got a pair of false eyes painted on me. Eyes with an unblinking, possibly harassing gaze that gets me hated or sucked up to.

Anyway, lockdown started, and the "what are you seeing" stuff got worse; the friends and family I video-called would get jumpy and nervous and ask why I was staring at the space behind them with this "shaman look" . . .

Everybody who had to sit alone with themselves during lockdown probably built an intricate nest of diseased thoughts around them, but these were mine: It seemed to me that I'd been built for a purpose I want no part of. I disliked the blanks in me; I think if an online user account created specifically for leaving nasty comments underneath other people's photos and articles gained sentience, it might feel the way I felt during lockdown. I washed and washed, and it helped to reduce that sense of expelling some sort of distressing pollutant without any idea of how to rein it in. I stopped video calls, but kept up with written messages and phone calls. I beefed up my cleansing procedures, from washing individual strands of hair to scrubbing between toes.

I fled my home as soon as it was safe to do so. A lot of people did. I could spot my fellow jjimjilbang nomads a mile away. We're the ones who switch our street clothes for the spa-provided T-shirt and shirts as quickly as we can, and we take the longest to relinquish our uniform when it's time to go, easing our feet out of those soft white slippers and back into those germ vehicles with pavement-soiled soles . . . ugh. I fell into this lifestyle like it was a feather bed. We're all the same here, every girl is just like all the other girls, regardless of age or anything else. Steam enfolds us, inexorable angels with loofahs and three-thousand-carat knuckles knead our muscles and peel our old skin away, naked, clothed and then naked again, we lie on warm stones with our souls swelling like the plumpest of yeast buns. Then we bathe again, anointing each other with waterfalls, and we head back towards the steam room. Rest and repeat, rest and repeat. No ritual sorts you out like the jjimjilbang rituals. Having met you at our favourite bathhouse, there's no need to persuade you of this, Haewon-ssi. But have you ever considered giving yourself over to the jjimjilbangs completely? Staying overnight at a jjimjilbang close to your workplace every night can be ever so slightly more affordable than monthly rent in outer Seoul, provided you pick establishments that offer the best value and also factor in loyalty discounts. All I had to do was reduce the bulk of my possessions so that they fit into a rucksack and a wheeled duffel bag—oh, and I had to keep circulating, so as not to overstay my welcome at any of my seventeen homes.

Hwang Violaine took her own path to jjimjilbang nomadism—I'm not sure if she told you about it. Somehow I doubt it. In order to know that story the two of you would've had to have a non-scripted conversation. Look, the main thing is that all three of us—you, me and Hwang Violaine—were checking in at that bathhouse at the same time. You saw Hwang Violaine, and, desperate to talk to her (I understand; that happened to me too, she's so very disdainful, it feels amazing when she lifts the VIP rope and lets you through), you hit upon the ruse of offering to take a photo of her and her friend.

"My friend?" Hwang Violaine asked. "What friend?" You meant me. I wasn't yet acquainted with Violaine, I was only queuing behind her. Actually I'd tried to speak to her a few moments before you approached us—we'd accidentally made eye contact for the second time in three days (I'd spotted her at another jjimjilbang two days prior) so

I said "Haha, hello again," but she'd only stared at me and said "What?" without taking her earphones out of her ears.

But when you offered to take the photo of us she took her earphones out of her ears, put her arm around me and told me to give you my phone. We posed as BFFs, for your benefit and ours too, I suppose. What to blame that on? Giddiness after years of having to shy away from strangers? The confidence of a jjimjilbang regular communing with another jjimjilbang regular?

So, Haewon-ssi, you gave me my phone back with your number saved as a contact, you returned to the queue for the men's area, and V told me she remembered me! "Same here," I said, thinking she was talking about the spa. But she was talking about a book signing she'd done years and years ago. She'd just given a reading from her latest book, the bookshop had been packed with literature fiends, she'd spent the next hour or so signing copies for everybody who asked. At a chance interval she'd looked up and seen me join the signing queue, an even longer line than this jjimjilbang one. At another chance interval she'd looked up and seen me shake my head, put her book back on the nearest shelf and leave the bookshop empty-handed. "Huh," I said. I'd forgotten all about it, but of course it all came back to me once she told me about it. She said she'd stored that sight away in her mind because it was humbling.

You facetiously asked what foundations people like us build our friendships on. For future reference, the answer is roasted eggs and the wisdom of ancients. Once we'd changed into our pale orange T-shirts and shorts, I tracked Violaine down and insisted on buying her dinner. She was all no, no, you don't have to do that, but now that we were in a photo together I felt bad about robbing her of a book sale.

V found a spot in the TV room with a good view of the screens, I joined her with a platter of eggs and two bowls of sikhye, and before we got stuck in, Violaine said: "First of all, Minjeong, let us pray."

She'd already fetched a book out of her locker—it was the Tao Te Ching. She raised it aloft and read aloud:

Nothing in all beneath heaven is so soft and weak as water.
And yet, for conquering the hard and strong, nothing succeeds
like water. And nothing can change it:
weak overcoming strong,
soft overcoming hard.
Everything throughout all beneath heaven knows this,
and yet nothing puts it into practice.

"But we will," I said.

"Amen," said Violaine. And on the count of three, we cracked our roasted eggs on our foreheads and fell to feasting.

I don't expect an answer to this, Haewon-ssi.

Look after yourself,
Kwak Minjeong

THE LANDLORD

Keith Ridgway

He came at the weekends in the afternoons, usually on Saturday, occasionally Sunday. He would leave his plump car glowing in front of the building, half on the footpath, half on the road. Once he came unannounced on a Friday evening, a little the worse for wear, and leaned heavily against the door jamb, struggling to write in my rent book, laughing about something behind me, or on my shoulder perhaps. Giggling. Just the once, this was, on a Friday. I watched him drive off and then come to a stop after only a few metres. The car crouched there like a dropped fruit, a lime from its tree, for example, or an unripe apple, and it didn't move, not until some other sort of car pulled up behind it and sounded a tentative horn. At which point my landlord, with a squeal of tyres, accelerated away at high speed.

In the summer he often came with his son, an over-weight boy of about twelve, who would cut the grass in front of the house while his father made his calls. The sudden noise of the lawn mower would rouse me, and I would glance out the window and see the boy, and the car, and go then and stand at the door to my flat and wait. Sometimes I put my ear to the door. Sometimes I put my forehead to it. I would at these times be tense in my body and vacant in my mind, as if there was nothing else I could possibly be doing. It was possible to estimate his proximity from the voices, the knocking, the noises, and it was possible to get it wrong.

I lived at the top of the house, in what was probably once an attic but which consisted then of a very small bathroom, a larger storeroom where the landlord kept old furniture and bits and pieces, and my single room with its broken bed, its table, a sink and cooker, a fridge and the chairs. Several chairs, only one of them comfortable. There were shelves on the sloping walls which could not bear the weight of more than a few dusty paperbacks and various mementos—photographs, little tins and boxes, my father's letters. The electricity came and went and in the summer the sun made the place impossible during most of the day. I would go to the park and walk there amongst the cool trees and see the swimmers in the lake and nod at men like myself who walked in the shade or lingered near the ruins of the old fort. In winter I would sit close to the gas heater.

He wanted always to talk. To take my money—the rent—of course, but also to talk, to pass the time, to ask my advice, to worry sometimes about his son, the boy in the garden, but more often to talk about his wife.

Sometimes it was the mower I heard first. Usually though it was the front door slamming in a way that was distinctly his. *Slamming* is too strong a word. A door let go, not closed. Not careless, but not entirely careful. The tenants closed the door. He let it go, with perhaps a small push of his hand, perhaps a couple of fingers. Then the loud, no-nonsense knocking at other doors as he made his way upstairs. I had the top-floor flat, as I say, at the front. I could see the road, the garden, the path, the first of the steps. I was rarely taken by surprise. I've said that. The car sometimes, the boy's voice, the lawn mower, the letting go of the front door, the knocking. And I would stand waiting. Sometimes I might drift off, and the knock then came like blows against the body, and I would flinch, winded for a moment, as if toppled while out on the wide grass.

I wanted nothing more than a place to live, you understand, nothing other than a place to be.

I was terribly timid as a child. My father raised me. He was a gentleman. Overly gentle, I would say. He has left me also gentle, and afraid sometimes. Fearful. Which people find unattractive in a man. I played sport, was good at football, and I swam. But as I grew older, my health. Now I walk. I walk great distances. And when I can, when there is no one to be seen, I run.

His voice at other doors seemed brusque. Occasionally raised. What my neighbours did to displease him I have no idea. I rarely spoke to them. But with me he had a quiet, respectful tone. He mispronounced my name. But he did it consistently and confidently, so that after some time I began to suspect that his pronunciation was correct and mine was not. At first he would just stand at the door. Lean sometimes against the jamb. He would greet me smiling and I would hand him my yellow rent book, the bank notes inside, marking the page. He would always deftly, quickly, with two or three fingers of one hand fan out the notes to count them, and fold and vanish them, content. He would write then in the book—the date, the amount, his initials—and hand it back to me. All the time talking, speaking, saying my name, flitting his eyes over my shoulder at the room, at the heater in the corner and the stale bed, the shirts hanging mildewed on the rail, the journals and plates on the table, and at some point he began to ask to come in.

May I come in?

Sometimes it was to take some small piece of furniture out of the storeroom. Or to put something in there. A hat stand. A mirror. A rug rolled up and tied. Maybe that is how it started. Him rummaging around in there. Me offering him something. Would you like something?

May I come in?

My mouth opened and closed and I shook, I think, my head, not in refusal, but in that way we do, a lip distorted, a small shrug of the shoulders, men like me, as much as to say, of course, if you like, certainly, I suppose, if you really want to, I don't know why you would, but yes, I'm hardly going to say no, am I?, come in, come in, you own the place after all, and I stay here at your generous indulgence. Certainly, please, I apologise for the mess. There was never any mess. A chair. Please. Have a seat. Some tea? Some tea?

In the summer when it was very hot he would walk over to the window and look out at the boy mowing the lawn, and complain about the heat, and complain about the boy, and he would see all my windows open and turn down the tea and seem puzzled by something. He would turn down tea in the summer. But sometimes in the winter he would say yes, and he might have one sip or none but he never drank it all. I offered him food but he seemed to have no interest in food. He was stout nevertheless. A belly hung over his belt, and his head was fat, puffy, his hair hanging down at the sides, bald on top, turning from a dirty brown to a clean-looking silver. He wore shirts typically, never particularly clean, always a little tight, and trousers the same. He was not in any way a handsome or elegant man, but he did not seem to know this, and so carried himself confidently. In my room anyway. Coming up the stairs. In the house. In the garden. In and out of his car. Maybe there were places where his confidence dipped, I'm sure there were, but I have no access to places like that. Not then, not since. Places where you can come and go as you please, and hang pictures on the wall, and paint, or ask friends around for dinner or to stay. Of course my father, in his letters, upbraided me for this state of affairs, insisting that a lack of initiative on my part explained these deficiencies, that I was nothing if not to blame. The landlord was never so direct. He would ask me politely how my work was going, whether I had had any luck, whether the gods or the angels or fate or fortune had deigned to smile on me in some way, that sort of generic enquiry. Always enquiring, as if to enquire, why are you still here?

I used to think that he and my father would get on famously.

His wife, he told me, was terribly depressed. She waited by the window all day. He woke in the morning and found himself alone, and went downstairs and into the front room that overlooks the gardens, the gardens of their house, and his wife sat there, in an armchair she had turned around, looking out over the grounds, down the long driveway to the gate. She did not stir at his voice. She did not say anything as he placed his hand on her shoulder, but she put her own small hand over his, and gently squeezed it, and he was relieved that her hand was warm, relieved that she could bring herself to touch him, relieved and of course distraught. She told him to leave the door open. He went to the kitchen and made the boy his breakfast. He would not name his wife. Or his son. They were "my wife," "my son." He asked me what he should do, how he should get through to her. I asked him if something had happened to his wife, or whether her depression was—as can often be the case, of course— without discernible cause. He looked at me curiously. He ran his hand over his forehead and sighed. And thanked me for the glass of water and stood up to leave. Pausing at the door, he turned to me and said that I had asked a very interesting question, one that had not occurred to him, and that he would give it a great deal of thought, and he looked forward to seeing me the following week.

She was waiting, his wife, perhaps, for someone to call. Hence the chair at the window. Hence the long driveway, the grounds, some sort of tree, a large tree, around which a path, that sort of thing. Someone or perhaps anyone. I thought I might call. Or at least . . .

I wondered where they lived. I looked through the documents. Tenancy agreement, rental contract. Itemisation of property contents, fixings, fixtures, furniture and ambient status. Condition thereof. Non-alteration declaration. Schedule of payments. Deposit receipt. Conditions of forfeiture. Proof of entitlement. Proof of good standing. Responsibilities of tenancy. Break-clause parameters. I looked for an address. But there was nothing but my address. For my landlord just a name, a telephone number. His name, that ambiguity. I wasn't sure I was reading it correctly. And I had dialled the telephone number once, when the woman in the basement fell. When she fell on the steps that time. I don't know what I thought I'd say to him, but in any case the number was not in service. A voice said that, or something like it. This number is not in service. This number does not exist.

At least walk up their driveway. So that she would see me. A figure, slouching up through the rain, hunched, solitary, a foul smell in the garden, the corpse of some animal. Or in the sunshine, obscured by a parasol, moving slowly as if dragging a foot, as if injured, looking for somewhere to rest for a while, pausing to lean against the tree. The big tree. I was curious what would happen. She would gasp and rise and go to the door. His wife. Would he be in? No. She would gasp and rise and go to the door.

The door first of the room she was in, the door then of
the house. She would gasp and rise and go to the door.

You poor man. You are soaked. Come in. Undress. I
will dry you.

She wouldn't say that.

I have been waiting for you. I realise now that you are
a cripple, so I must I suppose not be angry with you and
yet I am. I have been waiting. Waiting for you and you
have taken up too much of my time crawling to my lair.

She wouldn't say *lair*. Why would she say *lair*? She
wouldn't say *cripple*. She would think it. But these people.

I have been waiting for you. My husband tells me that
you are an ideal tenant. He says that you pay your rent
every week in full, that you have never been late with a
payment, that you keep the flat in good order, that the
neighbours have made no complaints, that you do not
hang pictures or make noise or have a trail of people
coming and going at all hours, visitors, unsocial hours,
music, you do not have music, that there is very little evidence that you are there at all most of the time, perhaps
the glow of a light late at night, but dim, seen only from
across the street, not unattractive in a house like that,
better than a cold blank darkness in the upper windows,
and you sometimes leave it on, don't you? Overnight.
Why? Because you think that some sign that someone
lives there is good for everyone, good for my husband,
good for his investment, my son, good for my son, who is

my husband's chief investment, good for me, as my husband's beneficiary, good for your neighbours, not to live in a house that looks empty, and good for you, as a sign in the world that you are in the world. A simple sign. A low warm light. Some warmth. Let's not romanticise things. It is a single bulb that casts an orange sort of glow over your shelves and the black glass, the book you read, your plate and cup, your table top, your bedclothes, your skin.

She would praise me for my humility, my acquiescence, my gentility. The gentility I posses by virtue of her cushions, her throws, her paintings, her sets of crockery, her glassware, her cornices and rugs, her books, her cases of books, biographies of sporting people, politically successful people, actors and painters, dead saints. There are no living saints, she says, laughing, throwing back her head and laughing, a glass in her hand, a hand at her neck.

She raised her hand to my cheek. She placed a glass in front of me. Had me sit by her side. She asked me about my childhood. She told me about her charity work and asked me to praise her generosity, to say that it was extraordinary, almost shocking, that she would give so much of herself to those who were dying, to the orphans, to the innocent victims of the war in Europe. A war in Europe, she said, sadly, aping distress, shaking her hands and her head, imagine, can you imagine such a thing?

Why would I go there? Why would I sit on the tram?

On the bus. Why would I sit on the bus, the sun on the side of my face the whole way, why would I sit there against the glass, my shoulder against the glass, the sun on the side of my face, my clothes too warm? Why would I get off the bus and walk the miles down the lanes and the edgeless roads, pushed by the cars, the sun on my legs, my clothes not warm enough, bright rain blowing at me from the north and the sun never dipping, the sun ranting in my ears, why would I walk all that way, travel all that way, my stomach empty, my head thin, to their home? To the gate and the driveway, the solid gate, the sweeping drive, the path around the tree, the big tree, and my slouching into view like an old smell, an axe in my trouser leg, a knife in my sleeve. I can tie knots. My father in his letters asks me continually to tie knots. Her hand on her throat. He means that I need to make connections. That I need to establish ties with networks of people who may be able to help me to become . . . I don't know what he thinks. But he says "tie knots." His English was always poor.

Perhaps they would like me. He likes me. In a certain sense, he likes me. Perhaps I could live in their house, a painter. Perhaps I could paint forgeries for them. Imitations of great artists. A lost Soutine, a Schiele drawing, a sketch by Pascin. An arrangement. He would know a dealer in the city, or a string of other men, a route. A way of taking my product and placing it just so. Provenance, history, pedigree. All of these things, forged. Interesting word. I mean it in the sense of counterfeit. Forfeit, counterfeit. Perhaps we could come to some arrangement. In return for my health, my meals, a bed, a walk in the grounds.

The grounds would be abandoned. Their son, perhaps, mowing the lawn. A fat child. I wonder is there a daughter? He is the sort of man to leave a daughter at home with her mother, to bring only his son to collect the rents. Jesus gave comfort to the rent collectors. Or was it the tax collectors? It was the tax collectors, of course. Not even Jesus had time for the rent collectors. Perhaps they would think of me like that. As a sort of Jesus. A Christ of the landlords.

His wife, he tells me, is unwell. There is something wrong with her heart. It cannot go on. It has had enough. It is winding down like a clock losing time, slowly but surely becoming useless, unmoored, toying with hesitation and suspense, stuttering, slower and slower, seeming many times to stop, but going on, and on, fitfully and formlessly, etc. He uses this sort of language—the simile and metaphor and analogy—but is incapable of pity. His wife, he worries, will die. He asks me if I have lost anyone to death. Have you lost anyone to death? I shake my head. No one has died. No one. Older relatives I did not know. A grandparent I cannot remember. A woman in the neighbourhood when I was a child but I had never seen her, never known her. She was the mother of a boy who knew my friends but whom I did not know. I saw him once, afterwards, playing football, the boy with the dead mother. A pal pointed him out. I watched him for a while but he seemed no different to the rest of us, indifferent, tired. Death has not touched me. Perhaps that makes me useless to him. Or perhaps the inverse is true.

He sits in the chair, slouched, his shoulders slumped, his belly pushed out, his hands lying usually in his lap, his eyes on the table top, on me, on the walls, sometimes on the windows. He sits as if exhausted. And sometimes he yawns. His mouth opens in a slow rictus distortion of his doughy face. He has small eyes, a country accent. He seems sometimes to doze off. I sit as still as I can. I wait. His eyes droop and his head nods. He says nothing, just breathes, is almost completely still.

But what do you think, he says suddenly, of the international situation? It worries my wife. Everything worries my wife. He laughs, scratches the dry skin of his forearm. Everything worries her. Noise worries her and silence worries her and the war worries her but if she didn't have the war to worry about she would be worried by the fragility of the peace, or the peace itself would worry her.

All those men of fighting age, she would say. With no
fighting for them to do. That is a tinderbox, she would
say. All those young men not dying, being allowed to live,
in society, with no outlet. She would worry about that. If
not that, something else.

  When I met her first the worry was much smaller,
a much smaller, more personal thing. She would worry
about how she looked. She would worry about not hearing from me for a day or two. Imagine that. She would
worry about saying something stupid in company, about
her parents not liking me, about money, about our lack of
money in those days, it was no joke I can tell you, until I
learned the laws and got to know how they're made. I can
tell you it was hard times then, you wouldn't believe the
amount of worry that I had, real worry, not the idle, not
the juvenile, not the fripperies, the fripperous worries of
my darling wife, if only she'd known how worried I was,
she would have died then of worry, but maybe she picked
it up a little, from me, no man can conceal everything,
and I am no actor, I can tell you, I am a pretty open book,
I think you'll find, and until I learned the law and met my
local representatives, got to know the men in the party,
the women in the party, all the parties, the lawmakers,
got to know them, learned the ins and outs of the laws,
until I understood how to operate the machinery of the
law, the dials and switches as it were, like driving an
old—ha—Massey Ferguson, or breeding horses, esoteric

knowledge, well. Back then we had things to worry about but she worried about fripperies. Now we have nothing to worry about and she worries about war. I ask you.

Sometimes he pats his pockets. He rolls a little to one side and his hand pats his pockets. I think perhaps that he used to smoke. He pats his pockets, and rolls upright again. Never actually puts his hands into his pockets. Never does that. I can see the bulge of a wallet. His keys he puts on my table. A huge number of keys, more than there are flats in the building. His building. More than double, I would say. Perhaps he has another building. We sit and hear the sound of the lawn mower. If I pour him a glass of water he does not drink it. He wants to talk about his wife. He talks, and looks at the table top, at the walls, at the glass that makes the windows, at the cupboards, the sink, the door. He does not look at the bed.

One day he said that his wife might be dying. A hot day. The boy mowing the lawn, the flies on the glass, his water untouched. She was, he said, unable to move any longer. She needed care. He had to employ a person to come to the house every day to help her do various things. He was vague about it, waved his hand back and forth, then laid it again in his lap. A very hot day. He might need to hire someone to move in. To care for her around the clock. Two people, he supposed, or even three. Constant care.

Who knows if she's getting towards the end? The doctors don't know. They come and examine her and they are bloody useless, I tell you. So who knows? It could go on years. It could go on years but every time I get out of the car and look at the windows I wonder what I'll find. Who knows? Very weak. The cost of it all is preposterous really. Just at the moment. With the war. And the interest rates. Interest rates, of course. Inflation. My boy with his extra lessons, he has various issues. He's a smart lad but there are challenges. Ah well, I won't bore you with it. One thing after another. One thing on top of another. And I know of course that you're not, that you yourself, you're not, of course, well, I know that, of course. But nevertheless. So starting from next month. Is it next month?

He looked at his wristwatch. And told me that from next month the rent would be raised by such and such an amount per week. He said, looking around, that he would have the place painted. Painted and cleaned. Don't worry about it, he said. Cleaned and painted, he corrected himself. I'll sort that out for you no bother, don't worry about that at all, a lovely fresh coat of paint. I'll have a man come to you with colours.

It's all, he said, very depressing. I mean the situation. With my wife. She's lost a lot of weight. I'd say more than twenty kilograms. In the last few months. Well, I know it is twenty-four kilograms, just under three months, I know it's that, there's no guessing about it. I put her on the scales myself, every Wednesday. We weigh ourselves every Wednesday. She started that. Ages ago now. Keeping an eye on my belly, got the weighing scales. Insisted I weigh myself every Wednesday, and she joined in herself, a little bit of encouragement for me, and sure enough when you see the numbers it becomes a challenge. I like a bit of a challenge. Nothing too serious. Just keeping an eye on what I eat after that. Lost a little. She never had to. But she's losing it now, let me tell you. She's a featherweight now, my god.

He rubbed his hands over his face and told me he'd be in touch about the cleaning and the colours and the painting, and off he went.

I am not myself, entirely. How could I be? I am something else. I am an allocated life—here you are, live here. I am a permitted sort of person. Here, stand here. Sit here. Lie here. Walk here. A tenant. Do you see? Nothing I can do about it now. My father dead, the empty shelves, the old house long lost, and the open fields, the sky. Nothing I can do about it now. In the end he found some anger. A little rage at the end. I stood embarrassed at the foot his bed, the nurses giggling, his skin turning purple and his breath loud amongst the machines, the beeping, the smells, the giggling. Never myself. Some other, measured thing.

I went to the place where they lived. I simply asked him one day. Do you have far to go? He said a place on the edge of the country. A townland. And I went there, a tram then a bus, not knowing exactly where the house might be. I wore a hood, a pair of shoes, some sunglasses, the coat. The heat was tremendous, and a group of police officers sat around on the main street, indolent, staring, eating sandwiches and drinking from cans, caressing those yellow sticks they always carry. I found the post-master but could think of no way of asking what I needed to know. Where does this man live? This, I think, being his name. I don't know how to say it. He drives this car. A son, a wife. I wandered out into the lanes and the roads. A distance in all directions. I stared at the big houses, the small houses, looking for his car. A fat boy mowing the lawn. A woman at the window. You know what I know. I thought once or twice that I saw him, or his son, but these people are everywhere. People like these. We have our laws, our lawmakers, our large estates, our country, our time. But it is *our* that is the lie, of course. Of course it is, you don't need me to tell you that.

I saw the car then. The unripe berry of his car, glowing cold on the ground between the hedges and the grass by the solid old stone of a mid-sized house, bow windows, a wide door between potted trees, a smokeless chimney, a still air, the scent of little apples, little limes, hidden. I stood and stared, my head on my shoulders. A gravel driveway. An iron gate, open. No path. No tree. Just hedgerows and empty beds, an agitation in the dusk that vanished when the eye sought it out. The windows all were empty. Blank and dark. I took several careful turns around them, and walked then, quickly, briskly, to the door and knocked. Or did not knock at all. Then I turned, ashamed, went back to the gate. Quickly. No sound. I went on. I went on to the corner where the lane turned towards the town. Quickly. I passed a frightened man, a running child. I ran myself. I found a meadow and galloped, a bridled man, yearning I suppose for some space unlimited by others, and behind me across the wide grass I saw the police officers go into the landlord's house, and come out again immediately, shouting and pointing, and they mounted their raging horses and set off in my direction, yellow flashes in their raised fists.

APOSTROPHE'S DREAM

Yiyun Li

CHARACTERS

A small cluster of movable type, all of them punctuation marks, including:

COMMA, PERIOD, COLON, SEMICOLON, QUESTION MARK, EXCLAMATION MARK, ELLIPSIS, HYPHEN, EN DASH, EM DASH, PARENTHESIS (a pair, P1 and P2), QUOTATION MARKS (two pairs: Q1 and Q2 are double quotation marks; Q3 and Q4 are single quotation marks), APOSTROPHE, and a few others.

They all have the same square, antique, and smudged appearance. One has to look closely (and, for an inexperienced observer, to seek assistance with a mirror) to identify them correctly.

Their speaking voices vary but have the same dull metal timbre.

They have been friends all their lives, living in close quarters in a typesetter's drawer. They have some acquaintances: letters in both upper case and lower case, but letters, though profoundly superficial, tend to act profoundly literate; and numbers, that most pompous band of brothers, who are good at inflating their values.

Punctuation marks are known for their acute sense of position, precision, and purpose, which is sometimes threatened by the world at large that is prone to imposition, imprecision, and purposelessness/fake purposefulness.

Curtain rises. An uncluttered space. Dusk. An etching of a Gutenberg press is barely visible on the wall. The types are sitting in an imperfect circle, reminiscent of Alice and her friends at their infamous caucus race.

COLON Attention, please.

The punctuation marks are talking with and over one another. No one seems to hear COLON.

COLON May I have your attention, please?

ELLIPSIS You're repeating yourself.

COLON It's my job to direct attention.

ELLIPSIS If you truly want attention, you should say something unexpected.

COLON Like what?

ELLIPSIS Like this. (*In a voice that must be raised for* ELLIPSIS, *which still sounds subdued*) Inattention, please, may I have your inattention?

No one gives their inattention to ELLIPSIS.

Yiyun Li

COLON If they don't give you their attention, how can you expect them to give you their inattention?

ELLIPSIS But I thought our discussion today was about the world's inattention to us. To understand others' inattention, we must understand our own first.

COLON I'm afraid that's not how the world operates.

ELLIPSIS How does the world operate?

COLON The world operates on misunderstanding, not understanding, and pretend-understanding.

ELLIPSIS I don't believe you. How do you know?

COLON I simply do. Don't forget that I often preside where officiality is needed, while you, my dear friend, you never have a chance to study the world.

ELLIPSIS I mingle with poets, and you must allow that poets know the deeper truths of human hearts.

COLON Poets? They are hardly our friends. They cannot afford to be.

ELLIPSIS Why not?

COLON Can they afford to pay attention to us? Can they afford to pay for anything these days?

ELLIPSIS Attention is not money.

COLON Shhhhhh. Don't let others overhear you. That alone will mark you as antiquated. And irrelevant. Attention, just so you know, is money these days. (*Not giving* ELLIPSIS *an opportunity to counterargue,* COLON *raises his voice again.*) May I have your attention, please?

> *Various conversations continue.* ELLIPSIS *walks around the circle, stopping next to each of the punctuation marks and scrutinizing them. By and by the circle, discomfited by the too-close attention from* ELLIPSIS, *turns quiet.*

COLON Attention, my friends.

ELLIPSIS (*refrains from speaking, and then to himself*) Ah, the lost art of omitting the obvious . . .

COMMA (*overhears* ELLIPSIS) I hope this is not the first time you recognize your existential crisis?

ELLIPSIS . . . ?

COMMA   Stating the obvious is one of the surest ways to stay relevant, in case you forget.

ELLIPSIS   I didn't forget . . . only because I didn't know. And surely that is not true. If relevance is about stating the obvious . . .

EXCLAMATION MARK (*thundering*)   Surely it is true!

>   **ELLIPSIS** *frowns, and then retreats to a corner, nursing his silence.*

COLON (*to the circle*)   Ah, yes, friends, let me remind you all: we have been discussing the pressing issue of relevance. We are, unlike letters and numbers, increasingly facing a fate of being misused, abused, and worse, rejected as being superfluous.

PERIOD   Words and numbers will disagree with that statement. I'm around them often. They complain about being misused and abused.

COLON   But they haven't yet been discarded as useless, have they? We contend with the fate of being erased.

QUOTATION MARK (QI)   Some of us have been plagued by our erasability for years now . . .

QUOTATION MARK (Q2) . . . and yet we have stayed unflappable and prevailed.

COMMA (*to no one in particular*) Tell that to my Oxford cousin—he's the most unflappable creature but that doesn't help in his case. Half—no, more than half—of the world don't even know of his existence these days.

QUOTATION MARK (Q3) As long as words think of themselves as important and quotable, we shall believe in our relevance . . .

QUOTATION MARK (Q4) . . . just as we shall trust the necessity of punctuation as long as words don't want to lose their sanity.

PERIOD (*to* QUESTION MARK) Do you think they ever speak without finishing each other's sentence?

QUESTION MARK I'm afraid that is not a legitimate question.

PERIOD You haven't realized that illegitimate questions are what carry the world these days?

QUESTION MARK I know that reality more acutely than anyone. Rhetorical questions are annoying enough to test one's endurance, but oh, the agony and the embarrassment of those illegitimate questions! Empty questions wearing the emperor's new clothes. Convictions posing as taunting questions. Questions that should rather end with you-know-who (*pointing to* EXCLAMATION MARK, *who is excitable, so it is wise not to mention his name*). What happened to the good old times when real questions begot real answers?

PERIOD   Or real answers begot real questions. I suppose people like statements more than questions now.

QUESTION MARK   Which means you don't really have to worry about being made redundant.

EXCLAMATION MARK   Neither do I!

SEMICOLON   Please lower your voice. You always give me a headache.

EXCLAMATION MARK (*whispers loudly to* HYPHEN, *who happens to be sitting next to him*)   What a grump he is! He doesn't know he's caused more headaches than any one of us.

HYPHEN (*morosely*)   I wish I were in his shoes. I wish I were as learned as he is.

EXCLAMATION MARK   Learned, my ass!

HYPHEN   But look at it from my angle. I am a joiner, Semicolon is a joiner, too. Nobody takes him for granted as they do me.

SEMICOLON *(who has been paying close attention to this side discussion)*   And yet you are at no risk of going extinct. You see, I work like a logician; you work like a welder. The world can make do without me, but not you.

HYPHEN   You are being an elitist. And you have no right to be.

QUESTION MARK   Might it be that he confused you with your cousins, Em Dash and En Dash?

SEMICOLON   I am not confused. It's not my job to be confused.

HYPHEN *(whispering to himself)*   Aye, it's your job to be confusing.

COLON   Attention, friends. To proceed efficiently, we need to establish an order.

PARENTHESIS (P1) We second that. Orders (established or unestablished or incapable of being established) have always been our *raison d'être*.

PARENTHESIS (P2) And yet we feel that it is important to remember that the world is not run on orders, but on disorders (some of them are stabilized, others are destabilizing).

COMMA All these parentheticals! I motion for a simpler discussion.

SEMICOLON As befitting your lightweight status.

APOSTROPHE (*clears throat and speaks with pauses and hesitation*) Friends, uh, friends, if you kindly allow me to put in a few words—I won't take long, I won't put in too many words—but with your kind permission, I recommend that we confront our dilemma collectively, rather than emphasising our individualities.

QUOTATION MARK (Q1) Already that is a statement erring on being exclusive. We (*pointing to* Q2) neither emphasize nor care for individuality.

QUOTATION MARK (Q2) We recognise the merit of duality and dualism.

EXCLAMATION MARK Quiet! Let Apostrophe speak!

APOSTROPHE Thank you, thank you, my friend. (*To* QI *and* Q2) I apologize to you. I've been taught by my grandfather and my father that our job is to shorten rather than to lengthen, to contract rather than to expand, and sometimes when a thought becomes a shortcut, precision is at risk.

COLON Kindly proceed to the point.

APOSTROPHE Yes, yes, let me be quick before more mistakes and more opinions arise. Sometimes when your job is to be brief in your worldly presence, you tend to be expansive in your dreaming. I hope I'm not alone in this . . .

EXCLAMATION MARK Some of us never have the luxury of time to dream! We are on call around the clock!

ELLIPSIS (*to himself*) I don't see the point of speaking aloud any dream.

APOSTROPHE Yes, thank you all for your opinions. I promise to be quick. I've been pondering the problem of staying relevant. It behooves us to remember that there was a time when words existed without us . . .

ELLIPSIS   And one day they will do so again . . .

EXCLAMATION MARK   Nonsense! The words would run on so without us! The world would be pure chaos without us!

PERIOD   Without me, perhaps, but I would say the world would be a saner place without keeping someone like you on call twenty-four-seven.

APOSTROPHE (*cutting in lest more opinions arise, and speaking more eloquently*)   You see, this is precisely the problem. We tend to emphasize our individual roles, and that's a caucus race that goes nowhere. What I would like to suggest is that we ought to think of ourselves as a unit and take up a noun collectively. For instance, porpoises and fish go by schools, which automatically requires some respect from unschooled minds. A shiver of sharks and a murder of crows send a chill down anyone's back. A thunder of hippos and a pride of lions cannot be ignored. A parliament of owls and a wisdom of rooks come with their innate authority. I think it would bring us some overdue attention and respect if we can settle for a good collective noun. For instance, a wisdom of punctuation marks.

QUOTATION MARK (Q1)   That feels like plagiarizing.

QUOTATION MARK (Q2)   Unless we put a pair of quotation marks around the word *wisdom* to acknowledge the borrowing. Though that could easily take up a hint of mocking.

QUOTATION MARK (Q3)   Which would turn us into a foolery of punctuation marks. Since I'm the one to say it aloud, why not call ourselves a foolery of punctuation marks?

QUOTATION MARK (Q4)   It has a nice ring, quite Shakespearean.

QUESTION MARK   What about a drift of punctuation marks? I always like when people get the drift of something . . . it makes my job easy.

SEMICOLON   Too flimsy; too insubstantial; too self-defeating.

PERIOD   Besides, a drift of anything belongs to the

officialese of letters. They like to create drifts—often imprecisely. We like precision.

QUESTION MARK An equation of punctuation marks? An ordinal of punctuation marks?

PERIOD If you want to hear the protest from numbers. And they have infinite ways of protesting.

PARENTHESIS (PI) An embrace of punctuation marks?

PERIOD Too familiar.

COLON A bearing of punctuation marks.

EM DASH A procession of punctuation marks.

EN DASH A run of punctuation marks.

COMMA A senate of punctuation marks, a brotherhood of punctuation marks, an ensemble of punctuation marks.

PERIOD No, all those words have their indefensible flaws. We should call ourselves a community of punctuation marks. I've noticed that *community* is a versatile word these days. Invincible, too.

QUESTION MARK   You may as well add an impact of punctuation marks, a synergy of punctuation marks, a strategy of punctuation marks, an alignment of punctuation marks, a challenge of punctuation marks, an authenticity of punctuation marks. They are all popular words these days.

SEMICOLON   I object. They are enough for me to think that we should just bow out of history and leave the words tangled in their stupidity.

COMMA   Maybe we should go for the obvious ones. No one can argue against the obvious.

QUESTION MARK   Such as?

COMMA   A hope of punctuation marks. A love of punctuation marks. A solidarity of punctuation marks. An empowerment of punctuation marks.

A long, long pause.

HYPHEN   A caution of punctuation marks. A warning of punctuation marks.

ELLIPSIS   We will never come to an agreement . . .

HYPHEN   A gaggle of punctuation marks. A squabble of punctuation marks.

PERIOD   Let's stop. This is a fool's errand.

COLON   And yet it's no more a fool's errand than other worldly proceedings, which begs the question whether we are not foolish enough.

ELLIPSIS   I have a proposal . . .

COMMA   Don't propose. I can always offer a different proposal, whatever you propose.

ELLIPSIS   . . .

PERIOD   . . .

QUESTION MARK   . . .

HYPHEN   . . .

Dusk has turned into night. The Gutenberg press blends into the grey background.

ELLIPSIS (*to self*)   I've never felt so relevant as at this moment.

APOSTROPHE   Apostrophe!

EXCLAMATION MARK   It's not your job to be excitable.

APOSTROPHE   I apologize. Only I think I've found a solution. Since it's unlikely that we can come to an agreed collective noun for ourselves, we should follow an age-old practice and call ourselves an apostrophe of punctuation marks, just as Newton's laws of motion or Euclidean geometry.

PERIOD   Aha. That's your plan all along, isn't it, to put yourself into a position of leading us?

EXCLAMATION MARK   This is preposterous!

APOSTROPHE   Allow me to elaborate, friends. There is nothing preposterous with my idea. How did the history of punctuation marks begin? It was the need for some space between words and sentences. We are, in the end, a collective of placeholders.

QUOTATION MARK (Q1)   A placeholder of punctuation marks?

QUOTATION MARK (Q2)   That sounds redundant.

APOSTROPHE   Any noun that goes before our names would be all right, as theoretically it's only a placeholder. In that sense an apostrophe of punctuation marks is as good as any other possibility. I've always dreamed of being a little more important than my puny self allows, so, my friends, why not indulge me for once, since the original idea is mine?

QUESTION MARK   Is there a term to your position?

COLON   We should establish an agreed term. It can't be like a chief justice of some court.

SEMICOLON   Or royalty.

PERIOD   And we should establish an order of rotation so we each can have our names used. A period of punctuation marks—that sounds rather appealing, don't you think? With a nostalgic tone.

EM DASH and EN DASH (*nodding at each other*)   And we will ask for a double term. A dash of punctuation marks!

> *An eruption of different voices from around the circle. Curtain falls while the conversation continues.*

HEADACHE

Leone Ross

The letter about the orgasmic headaches arrives through her door at 10.37 p.m. and Kinshasa Cabral is momentarily puzzled. Then she opens it, remembers, sucks her teeth, and shows it to her boyfriend, Noah Golden. He's fresh out of the shower, sitting on the side of her bed, cocoa-buttering.

But that was a year ago, he says, turning the flaccid letter over in his hands.

Yes, says Kinshasa Cabral.

She remembers the onset: Noah Golden was nestled between her thighs, doing something helpfully repetitive with his tongue, when a terrible heat rippled up her back and into the nape of her neck. On climax, she felt as if her forehead was melting and clutched her skull, unable to speak for several agonised minutes, barely registering Noah's hands cradling her.

When the awful headache happened five times in succession, Kinshasa described the symptoms minutely to a grey-eyed doctor who was visibly uncomfortable at her candour. Barely thirty, Kinshasa has never been sick enough to develop a relationship with a doctor, but she enjoys precision. She likes that Noah Golden nurtures ghost peppers and white roses on his apartment balcony; she likes transferring grades from emails to spreadsheets for examination boards at the university where she has worked for a decade. She likes crossword puzzles and mystery novels. She loves watching her best friend, Monica, knit soft, peachy shawls. She should have known something would go astray with this doctor, squinting at her notes, remarking that Kinshasa's symptoms were unusual. What gone bad a-morning can't go good a-evening, Kinshasa's mother likes to say, and she's quite right. The shirking doctor said she would refer Kinshasa Cabral for a brain scan, but no letter had arrived, and the headaches went away as quickly as they came. As the weeks passed, they'd returned to their usual lovemaking, all chuckling kisses and Noah's pubic bone in just the right place, although at first he found it difficult to orgasm himself, because he was worried about hurting her.

✦

Bright and early, Kinshasa calls the doctor to say she doesn't need the scan anymore. The receptionist says he wouldn't know about that. Can I speak to someone who does know, says Kinshasa Cabral politely, but the receptionist says call the hospital where the scan is scheduled. Kinshasa and Noah Golden go to carnival and whine-up and laugh with their friends, who have got to know each other in the past two years of their dating and like each other as much as can be expected. One of Noah's people says carnival has changed and he feels objectified; Kinshasa Cabral says he's dressed in huge red and blue feathers and a diamanté G-string to play mas, so he can't be surprised people are looking. That's not what I mean, says Noah's friend, and looks at her hard, but she is too busy with a bottle of Red Stripe and laughing with Monica and Gracie who she's known since school uniform days.

She calls the hospital three times from work, waiting 47 minutes, 31 minutes, then nearly an hour on different days. Monica says she should just go, because there's 7.7 million people on waiting lists and the delay on the scan doesn't make it unnecessary. Kinshasa says the lack of headaches makes it unnecessary. She understands bureaucracy: if she can just find the right administrator she'll get a box unticked or a screen changed in no time. But she has no success. Nine days later, she finds herself in a congested waiting room, wedged between a sleeping drunk and a chatty woman with three small, freckled, galloping children. The mother is in a scarlet frock and broken fishnet tights and looks surprisingly well rested. Kinshasa feels distracted and tired. She has been dropping things all morning, her black shoes, her purple handbag, the lucky blouse she planned to wear, straight into a puddle on the floor of her kitchen, because she'd left the freezer door open and the ice melted.

The children bounce off the slick walls, like ping-pong balls. They're Maisie, Kirkland and Anastasia, says the mother, as if anyone's interested. Kinshasa Cabral nods politely. There is a clock that ticks and orange posters on the walls about IUDs. The red-frocked mother asks if she's here for something bad, and Kinshasa says no. It isn't syphilis or something, is it, says the woman, hunching forward, and Kinshasa says she'd rather she didn't guess, thank you. Oh God, says the mother, it's something *really* bad, isn't it, I'm so sorry. She doesn't look sorry, she looks inquisitive. It's just a mistake, says Kinshasa. It's an MRI I don't need anymore.

They never make that kind of mistake, says the mother.

The drunk laughs, like a man not quite right.

For the first time, Kinshasa is more worried than annoyed. Maybe she does have something unusual. A brain scan is quite a scary thing. She should have asked Monica or Gracie to come along and be with her. Her father would have taken a day off from the electric shop. The red-frocked mother says if it's serious, Kinshasa's bound to lose all her amazing hair. She beckons to her children, twisting themselves across the shiny floor, pretending to be eels, and points and says, isn't her hair special, Maisie? So tall. Yes, of course you can come and look at her, you don't mind, do you? The girls trundle forward, little fists outstretched.

Kinshasa excuses herself to the bathroom.

Inside, she pats the braids piled on top of her head and washes her hands slowly. When she comes out, the freckled family is gone and a radiographer with a chart is saying Kinshasa Cabble, is Miss Cabble here? She has a kind expression and pink scabs on her knuckles.

Kinshasa pronounces her name correctly.

The woman's peeled face glimmers like a white boiled egg. She says please follow me and sets off at a clip; Kinshasa skips to keep up. They walk down a long corridor, the hum in the waiting room abruptly cut, like a television snapped off. The eggy radiographer says Kinshasa will be changing into a gown, removing everything but her underwear, no bra, no jewellery. Kinshasa asks if she can just have a word about this, because it's possible none of it is necessary. The radiographer says Kinshasa should place her belongings in a locker and wait for a while, she'll come back to get her when the scan room is ready. Kinshasa says she doesn't have symptoms anymore. Eggy beams and says that's wonderful, and here's the changing

room, and can she change into a gown, removing everything but her pants, no bra, no jewellery. Kinshasa blinks.
They are both repeating themselves. The scabs on the radiographer's hands are raw in the white light. She should
wear gloves. Eggy says she should pin her locker key to
her gown, and Kinshasa gives in and strips and changes
and makes small, precise movements, which helps when
she can't take charge of bigger things. She sits in an icy,
empty room and counts the chairs during the while that
is longer than a while should be. Her blue-and-white
gown flaps open at the back. Her bare feet are cold on
the floor. She's sure that one of her nipples is lower than
the other, evident through the thin material.

The radiographer comes to get her, smiling warmly. She
says it's so nice to see her again, Mrs Cabble, and Kinshasa says Cabral and Miss, please. Eggy smiles and says,
oh that doesn't matter, and Kinshasa doesn't know how
to reply. The scanner looms: a huge, white, sausagey con-
traption, bigger and older than the picture in the pam-
phlet that came with the letter. Kinshasa's glad it's just
her head going in: it'll be hard enough stopping herself
jerking or shouting or sneezing or laughing involuntarily.

The radiographer pats the flat bed attached to the
machine, inviting her to lie down. There is a wedding
ring on her left hand, past the swollen scabs. Kinshasa

lies down. Eggy says she will be inserting a cannula into Kinshasa's arm so that a contrast agent, a kind of dye, can be run intravenously. The dye might cause a warm and tickling feeling during the scan, she says. People think they've wet themselves, but Kinshasa mustn't worry, it's a common sensation.

Kinshasa tries to relax. Perhaps this can be interesting if she lets it. She asks what colour the dye is, trying to sound playful. Eggy says it's usually blue, but that a different colour is necessary for patients like her, and also she can play some music while Kinshasa is inside the machine, what does she want, Tina Turner's "Nutbush City Limits" or Annie Lennox's "Sweet Dreams" or "Ain't Nobody" by Chaka Khan? Kinshasa doesn't understand what she means by a different colour dye for people like her, and also those three songs are her mother's favourites. She plays them all the time, Annie, Tina, and Chaka, the poetry powerhouses, Mamma calls them, strutting her way around the large kitchen, Pops looking on fondly.

She likes thinking of her parents. They are mostly happy.

The radiographer says, song? song? you can only have one and scrubs the inside of Kinshasa's elbow for the cannula. Kinshasa says, Tina Turner, and can you be a bit gentler, please? Eggy folds Kinshasa's hands over her belly, her fingers clammy. She says lie still and that there's a sharp scratch coming up: she pushes the cannula into the back of Kinshasa's hand, where the skin feels like tissue paper. Kinshasa inhales and says ouch. The hand throbs, unprepared; why did she clean the elbow, then? Eggy says there'll be a banging sound once the scan begins, but it's nothing to worry about and if Kinshasa needs anything, at any time, just say so, she can hear her out here.

Deep breath, she says, and pushes Kinshasa all the way into the chute, up to her toes.

Her entire body.

What, says Kinshasa. She taps the shiny surface above her, fast and then faster and says, hello, I'm all the way in.

The silence is heavy and dry and there's salt on her tongue.

Hello?

Kinshasa breathes in through her nose and out through her mouth and thinks about sitting curled up to Noah Golden, in his shade, they always joke, he so big and she so small. The chute is old and white, and she can see rust and is afraid of the rust. She calls out again, can anyone hear me? The radiographer's voice says, all well? and Kinshasa says, no, I'm not supposed to be all the way *in*, and the radiographer says, I'll play you Chaka Khan very soon, and Kinshasa says, I'm not supposed to be all the way in, and I said Tina. The hair at the nape of her neck pulls, and she lifts her head to relieve the stretch and Eggy clicks in to say "Ain't Nobody" is coming up but you have to hold very still and Kinshasa thinks that Chaka Khan instead of Tina isn't so bad.

The tube is curiously inert. Even the quietest of machines hum, but this one feels . . . dead. She half-expects the radiographer to say it isn't working, to apologise, to say that's why she can't hear her, why the system only plays one song, why her whole body is inserted.

She can hear giggling. Through the silence.

Hello? Her voice squeaks.

The chamber bursts into banging, much louder than she'd feared, jerking her body upwards, belly arcing, the whites of her eyes flooding with bright, dead light. She fights an urgent, spreading need to urinate.

Seconds later, the chute pushes her body forward and out and she thinks, breathe, that wasn't so bad. The radiographer pops up at her side, beaming. Kinshasa's head weaves and she can see strange white twinkling lights in front of her face.

Eggy tells her that she is absolutely *beautiful*.

Hot shame fills Kinshasa: despite the woman's reassurances, she has wet herself.

She lived in another country as a child, one where dusk came at the same time every day, and where there were vultures and hummingbirds and women with fibroids the size of crocodile eggs. Her parents had been sanguine, thoughtful, almost communist, when she began to ask questions about where babies came from: they gave her books, they answered questions, they encouraged aunts and uncles to give educated, relaxed opinions. Over supper, the adults merrily debated what was better, sex in love or sex for fun, and concluded that both experiences were just as good as each other, provided you knew what you wanted.

Nobody else had an upbringing like hers.

Eggy coaxes her into a wheelchair and pushes her out of the scan room. Kinshasa feels light-headed and stinking. The cannula throbs inside her flesh. She asks where they're going, and Eggy says onto the ward for a clean-up and not to worry, the doctor will come very soon. Kinshasa doesn't understand. She needs a bathroom, a towel, her own clothes, yes, but the letter didn't say anything about a consultation. Has the radiographer seen something frightening on her scan? She thinks how quiet everything is in this place, and where is everybody? Eggy jams the wheelchair against shiny metal lift doors and crouches down beside her. Her small eyes are sad and blue. Kinshasa's belly lurches: she asks, is this normal, is there something to worry about? Oh no, says the radiographer, everything's fine. There are orange posters about condoms on the walls. Eggy slides her hand over the lift buttons and Kinshasa can't see the floor she punches.

The lift smells bad, sweet like a baby's vomit. She is aware of Eggy's body behind her, pressing lightly through the canvas of the chair, of the heat radiating out of her skin. Kinshasa edges forward, repulsed. The radiographer sings "Nutbush City Limits" all the way up to their floor. Kinshasa is surprised by her incredible voice: the metre and sweep make her think of Gracie's slow-simmer chocolate tea at Christmas. Eggy stops singing and says they'll be there soon; she picks her nose. When the doors slide open, she shoves the chair into the hands of a tall woman who is standing waiting at the lift door and takes a step back. She waves.

Here's the slut then, Eggy says.

What, says Kinshasa, *what* did you call me?

The new woman grasping the wheelchair says hello, I'm the Charge Nurse, and Kinshasa says, did you hear what the radiographer said, she called me a *name*?

We've been waiting all morning to meet you, says the Charge Nurse.

She has a small and clean private room: a rough blue curtain pulled around a crisp single bed, a low cabinet to her left, a seat for visitors and a large window that looks out onto the hospital car park. In the distance, she sees a twin set of tennis courts and the tops of warm green trees. She appreciates the reminder that there is light, and sunshine; the hospital is gum-dim, dead-coloured, like the scanner. She thinks of her valuables in the ground-floor locker, of her phone and silly, bright-coloured texts from her mother.

The Charge Nurse fusses about, encourages her to slip off her sodden underwear, wipes the urine off the wheelchair, hands Kinshasa a small, thin, wet tissue and a pair of paper pants. Clumsily, Kinshasa reaches beneath to wipe her thighs, uncomfortable under the woman's gaze. Why does she not look away? The tissue is not nearly enough; she asks for more. The Charge Nurse says yes, but it's good not to be wasteful. She hands over another single square. Kinshasa asks the Charge Nurse whether two thin squares would be enough for *her* if she *wet* herself. The Charge Nurse says everybody is very different and who knows the answer to questions like that. Kinshasa Cabral waits. The Charge Nurse pulls out two more squares, saying, very well, I'll spoil you then, enunciating loud and slow, as if they're not speaking the same language. Kinshasa wipes as much as she can: one thin ankle where the pee trickled and dried; her pubic hair.

The Charge Nurse rearranges the pillows, shows her how to remotely elevate the bed head and pull the table across her chest. Kinshasa asks if the doctor is coming soon and has the scan shown something, and why is she being settled down as if she's going to be staying? The nurse's lips puff out, as if insulted, and she says Kinshasa needn't be so sensitive. She picks up the anorexic Bible on top of the cupboard, clutches it to her bosom, as if protecting it, and says everything about those horrid headaches will be taken care of before Kinshasa leaves, this is the best hospital.

She knows she doesn't have orgasmic headaches anymore because she masturbates and her climaxes are easy, fast, pain-free, like old friends. She began when she was eleven. She still remembers the deliciousness of her self-exploration: the heavy falling asleep afterwards, the miraculousness of her growing body. Years later, when she begins to take lovers, she disrobes like a proud artist, spreading her wares to be admired. Noah watches her sometimes: it arouses him, her sharing, her efficient, slick fingers that he tastes afterwards.

An hour passes, perhaps. No clocks. She has no memory of the last time she sat in silence, with no book, no phone, no computer, no sound of neighbours or even birdsong. She's not sure what to do. The window is hermetically sealed; she can't hear the breeze or the tennis courts. She imagines the *clock!* sound of rackets, the grunts of the players; love. She wonders how she will respond to the bad news that might be coming; is she dying, does she have something that will cause her pain, make her ugly and sour? Will she be given medication? She hums old songs from old films, pops her lips: *pop-pop-pop*. Gets off the bed to stretch, to jump up and down on the spot. The thud of her feet; her soles are dirty, her thighs rub. She wishes she'd asked a friend to come and pick her up.

She sags with relief when the doctor arrives: he moves like the yellow, avuncular men in her family. She assumes he will recognise her too; will have memories of all-day cookouts and drum and bass, and laughter and sleeping on the pull-out, like her uncle Brian, who leads the breakfast arrangements with melting fried plantain made out of fruit gone black and the fluffiest scrambled eggs. The doctor will see she is somebody's niece and tell her the bad news gently. But he does not recognise her; he is snappish, almost angry. He has come, he says, with the forms she hasn't completed. He loads them onto her bed, sharp paper flowing over her hips.

There is a form about the circumstances of her birth, which requires a description of the hospital where she was born, and her parents' state of mind. There is a form asking about her medical problems from age zero to six, including how her cradle cap was removed from her soft scalp, how long it took her skull to shape itself pleasingly, daily reports of milk intake and the condition of her mother's aureole. There is a school form, she'll need all her school reports, and at least two interviews with childhood friends, reflecting on her personality. There is a menstruation form, asking for descriptions of her first, most recent and ideal period. There are more. Kinshasa's head whirs; her legs are string. She asks what the scan says. The doctor sits on the end of the bed as if tired and swings one of his legs, like a boy, and says he won't see her scan until tomorrow. Kinshasa says that she hasn't had a headache for nearly a year, no kind of headache at all, much less an orgasmic headache, and also says she can't fill in any of these forms, she doesn't understand why they are necessary.

The doctor sighs and takes her blood pressure, jerking her arm forward, rustling the forms, wrapping the sleeve too tight; it sucks at her arm like a leech. The reading is 157/93, the highest ever. The doctor tries to take blood, but the flow is sluggish through the needle, and he can't get enough. She asks if the cannula can be taken off the back of her hand, but he says it's necessary, she will have to be patient. He asks her how many lovers she's had, says the word like it's *livers* and she's confused; does he mean penetrative sex, or other sexual activity? He says she shouldn't be coy. How many, he says. She tells him

the heteronormative ones, counting on her fingers under the sheet. He says they'll check for diseases, and she
should make a start on the forms, and when she says she
needs to tell someone if she is staying the night, and what
diseases does he mean, he nods, as if that is an answer of
any kind.

Her first boyfriend in high school was lovely: their kisses
smelled of lemonade and he was solemn, almost breath-
less, when he first discovered her wetness. She thinks
that it was her optimistic sexual energy that sustained
her when he died of lymphoma at fifteen; the joy of her
young body kept her rooted and upright. She thinks of
herself as generally resilient. She spends her time organ-
ising people: ordering around brilliant and stupid aca-
demics alike. But now she is shocked at the feeling of
concrete in her bones. She has deflated, like a jellyfish,
here on this bed. She is sad to be here, thinking of that
first love and the room he died in, his bed decorated with
red balloons.

The early evening moves closer to the buildings, taking
away the light, pushing it behind corners and up against
walls. She is hungry and thirsty. She finds a small dusty
packet of gum in the bedside cabinet and sucks pieces,
slowly. A nurse brings a bottle of water, takes a swig before handing it to her, makes sweeping motions with her

hands, as if explaining drinking. The blonde hairs on her arms fizz in the unnatural light. She has a small nose ring. Kinshasa asks when there'll be food, and the nurse asks if she booked, and Kinshasa says well, no. The nurse lifts the forms off the bed and piles them on the table and says she understands, sometimes she gets busy too and forgets to prioritise, never mind, and Kinshasa snaps that she didn't know she was staying here and what the hell, can I have my phone, please, you expect me to stay here without food and nobody knowing I'm here? The nurse's eyes rim red, her mouth quivers, she says she's so sorry, she's had a long day, and Kinshasa reminds her of a friend of hers who didn't eat enough, and it's upsetting. She rearranges the forms on the table, sniffing. Her friend ended up sectioned.

Kinshasa sips her water. She must manage this.

She stares at the luminous clouds through the window. How has she not noticed the rain streaks across the glass, the flashes of wicked gold light? The muted rain is torrential. The bulbs in the car park make the trees look like ashy creatures, swaying in wind. She has dinner plans with Gracie and Monica tomorrow night at that cocktail place. Noah Golden will want to know how the scan went. She's playing dominoes with her father at his monthly tournament next week and he's coming over on Sunday to discuss strategy and bring pepper sauce. If her scan is bad tomorrow, then Pops can help her tell Mamma. Her hands feel dry; she reaches for hand cream, remembers that she has no bag.

She slips out of bed and out of the room, clutching the back of her too-small gown. The corridor echoes both ways. There is nothing here. Where is the nurses' station? She drifts to the left, past closed doors, hesitantly tries one. The room inside is empty, identical to hers. Kinshasa closes the door behind her. She thinks she hears voices somewhere. Her back prickles.

She returns to her room. She sits down on the bed. She takes a breath. It rains on. She wants to cry. She slips under the sheet and pulls it up to her chin. She should try the forms, if only to have something to do. But they haven't left her a pen or pencil. If the Bible were still here, she might have read it. She dozes. Tomorrow will be better.

The sky cracks, she hears that. The door batters open and she is awake, mouth leaking, wondering blearily if the storm has broken through the building. Pale nurses sweep in: six of them, three for each side, military precision. The Charge Nurse and Eggy, peering down at her; is that the red-frocked mother, the first, grey-eyed doctor? Kinshasa says, what, what, what, until one of them covers her lips with tape. They splay her like a butterfly. Six pairs of hands, twelve palms, sixty fingers, so much to bear she is retching. They rub and pinch, put their hands deep in her hair, pulling and twisting and patting, the way you might dig your fingers into an animal's pelt. They scrape their nails down her back, taking handfuls of her surface, as if she is an experiment, an unknown thing with acid in her veins. They hold her as if she is transformative: an ocean they expect to swell and fill the room, a being that might fly. They flip her, efficient and swift, like a stroke victim, as if they are here to bathe and dress her, but what they are doing instead is a kind of frenzy, rubbing and rubbing and rubbing her skin, calling between them: isn't it soft, isn't it soft? One nurse slurps at her fingers, as if tasting something luscious.

Kinshasa fights. She kicks one in the chest, so hard that the woman reels backwards, flailing through the curtain, tearing the material, half-exposing the bed. Kinshasa bruises them. She grasps a cheekbone, rips at a breast, they cry out that she is hurting them. She gets the pin with the locker key off the shoulder of her gown, but someone knocks it out of her hand.

Afterwards, she sits in the chair by the window.

Her people come to get her, the next day. She hears them, filling the corridor with noise, friends furling out behind

her mother like a bridal train. They gather around her
bed; they touch the curtain, horrified. They rip down
its ragged remains. Their shadows remind Kinshasa of
long and floating birds. They wrap her in a soft shawl, a
diaphanous cotton dress. Her skin hurts. Monica parts
her hair and oils her scalp. Uncle Brian fills the room
with music and the colours she likes: purples, lime green,
pink. Noah lays down a bowl of orange peel and ginger;
the scent covers them all; his face is inside out. Mamma
climbs into bed with her and touches her cheeks, her
hands. Her father weeps.

Enough, says her mother.

They consecrate this battleground. They draw her
back to them. And when she is ready, they take her out,
and away.

She has headaches, though, whisper the nurses, gathering to watch them leave. Bad headaches.

THIS FACT CAN EVEN BE PROVED BY MEANS OF THE SENSE OF HEARING

Charlie Kaufman

I. felt out of sorts, foggy and dull, the meat that was his brain was the wrong meat tonight, not his own. Someone else's meat, perhaps. It was a brain to which he did not have full access. He had some access. He could lift his arm if he wanted, for example, and did, just to prove it, but his thoughts were somehow hidden from him. It felt close in there, in this foreign brain, stuffed, warm and airless and, somehow, dusty. He imagined watching himself from the outside, sitting before this sad, small audience. As if seeing myself in the third person, he thought, although not exactly that, as he was seeing through his own eyes and therefore not seeing himself at all, the way one can't, which if he had been a person other than himself, a third person, he could have. It was perplexing. Of course, even in the first person he would be able to see his own body, the front of it, at least, as well as his face, were he to look at his reflection, which he couldn't now, as there were no mirrors at this venue, and, anyway, he would've avoided them if there were, as he was unhappy with his face; he thought it ugly, and so he was relieved to be on the inside looking out. Although he imagined he probably wouldn't much care that this face was ugly if it wasn't his. It was all perplexing. Furthermore, as far as the whole third-person notion went, I. was clearly not written by an omniscient narrator, if it could be said I. was written at all, but rather by a subjective one, or rather a group of subjective narrators, a world of them. For I. seemed able to glean truths about himself only via the assessments of others, or rather his interpretation of the assessments of others, to whose brains he also had no access. What do they think of me, he wondered, as he looked out at those present tonight who were, currently, not regarding him at all but rather watching the interviewer read aloud a passage from his novel. He couldn't hear her, or rather he couldn't focus on what she was reading. It seemed distant and garbled, as if she were reading underwater at the far end of a swimming pool. So he scanned the audience's faces. I. really wanted them to like this passage, whatever it was. But their faces were blank. They hate me, he imagined.

The interviewer finished, looked up.

"What exactly did you mean by that?" she asked.

As one, the audience's heads pivoted to I.

Oh.

It was his turn to speak.

They were six altogether, this audience: a strait-laced older woman in a knotted neckerchief; an effete, beret-wearing young man; a broad-shouldered tough in a tan sports jacket, whom I. suspected might be an undercover policeman; a sailor in dress whites; an angry-looking, raven-haired (possible dye job?) woman in a traditional folk costume (possibly Latvian?); and a heavy-set lady surrounded by several full garbage bags, whom I. figured was homeless and there only to escape the weather. The group waited, impatiently, it seemed to him, for his response, and he understood they hoped he would fail. People were sharks, pouncing if they sensed weakness. No, sharks don't pounce. And they sense blood, not weakness. His metaphor was off. This was just like him, he guessed. Still, it could be argued that excessive bleeding led to weakness, so perhaps a shark would indeed be able to sense—

The sailor coughed. I. was losing them. He hated the sailor most of all. Who did that sailor think he was in that stupid, impeccably tailored sailor suit?

"Could you repeat the question? I'm sorry. I was distracted. I had something in my eye. A crumb, perhaps," he lied.

"I asked, what did you mean by that?"

A silence.

"Yes. I see. Right. Of course," he said.

Another silence.

"By *what* exactly?" he asked.

"That passage."

I. nodded vigorously and for a long time, then said, "Might you reread the passage, then? I was distracted by my eye crumb. As you know."

This time, I. listened with laser focus.

"*Everyone carries a room about inside him. This fact can even be proved by means of the sense of hearing. If someone walks fast and one pricks up one's ears and listens, say in the night, when everything around about is quiet, one hears, for instance, the rattling of a mirror not quite firmly fastened to the wall.*"

The passage was completely foreign to him, as if he'd never heard it, let alone written it. Further, the idea expressed seemed insane, certainly nothing he would ever think. *We all have a room inside us?* I mean . . . Further, even the turns of phrase did not feel like his own. Although now that the idea of a room in one's head was put into *his* head, inside *him*, as it were, it did feel familiar and terribly upsetting. He worried this room idea would fester in him, grow like a fungus, a giant fungal chamber, shadowy, dusty, airless, and made of mushroom meat. Nothing good could come of this. He felt afraid. Further, what was with "*This fact can even be proved by*

means of the sense of hearing"? A stilted slog from one end
of that sentence to the other. Was his book translated
into English? Why would he have written it in another
language? He was unilingual, wasn't he? Yes, he was,
much to his embarrassment, and his unilanguage was,
of course, English, although he had purchased a Spanish
phrasebook just the other day or maybe last year in order
to better himself. "Oh, you must be an American, then,"
non-Americans always said to him when he, with embarrassment, admitted to speaking only English. And,
yes, they were correct. He was indeed an American, this
much he knew about himself. Although he didn't feel
like an American, or rather he didn't feel like what he
imagined it felt like to be an American. He imagined
Americans felt proud to be an American, or rather he
imagined that Americans who felt like an American
felt proud of it. He guessed there were a lot of Americans who felt ashamed to be an American who didn't
feel like the Americans who felt proud to be one. Maybe
there were some Americans who felt neither proud
nor ashamed to be an American but recognized it as a
mere accident of birth. That was, he decided, probably
the mental-healthiest way to look at being anything or
anyone. But he couldn't manage that sort of detachment
regarding this or any other of his attributes. He had to
be ashamed of it because there were so many people who
hated America, and justifiably so. So he was required by

his nature to direct their hatred inward. Perhaps he could just say to the interviewer, since he had to say something (fourteen eyes upon him), that he hadn't written that passage at all, that he would never write such a passage, and, in addition, in case anyone was wondering, he was ashamed to be an American. But how could he claim he didn't write it? She was reading directly from his book. *His* book equals *his* passage. Wait. Could it be a trick? A prank? No, she wouldn't do that. No one would do that. But then, he didn't really know this interviewer. At least he didn't think he did. Did he? His memory was failing him, that much he knew, or rather suspected. What if she were doing exactly that—a prank—and he were to fall right into her pranky trap by attempting to explain, as his own, this nonsensical passage which he hadn't written and never would? That could be career-ending, even in front of a tiny audience of seemingly insignificant people. Maybe the audience was even in on it. Maybe they were actors. They did seem an oddly caricaturish bunch, in their various costumes. If experience taught him anything, it was that real book launch audiences were non-descript—jeans and T-shirts, maybe a sundress or two in the warmer months, the occasional glowing pregnant woman in something midriff-baring. In any case, even if they weren't in on it, they would talk once the prank was revealed. People are out to get you. How could he possibly wriggle out of it when the interviewer revealed she had been pranking him? Could he say, "Yes, I know, and I was pranking you back? Psych!" No one would buy that. Perhaps he should ask to see the passage, then he could ascertain if it was indeed from his book and in the process buy himself a little time.

"May I take a look at that passage in your copy, *por favor?*" he asked, utilizing his Spanish while jabbing a brittle finger toward the interviewer's lap, where an open copy of his book lay, "To refresh my memory."

I. pictured how he must look from the outside, in the third person, as it were, speaking Spanish, pointing, and he worried it all appeared untoward, this aggressive bilingual stab of his finger toward her lap. It's not that he was sexually attracted to her, although it's not that he wasn't, and he did love women's laps. He couldn't say why, but he suspected it calmed him to lay his head in a woman's lap or to imagine doing so. Maybe it made him feel protected, the way laying one's head in one's mother's lap would. That was probably mostly it. Not that he had ever lain his head in his mother's lap. Theirs hadn't been that type of relationship, as far as he could recall, which was not far at all. His childhood seemed impossibly distant, a blur, viewed underwater at the far end of a swimming pool.

The interviewer handed her book to him, and he saw that, yes, it was exactly as she had read it. Could it be she had pasted a false page into his novel? But why, why would she do that? Why would anyone do anything like that? It seemed more likely that he had just forgotten writing it. His memory was going; he remembered that much. Then again, you never know with people, especially in the literary world. Literary people were sharks. Still, he had to proceed, to get through this interview. There was nothing else for it.

"Ah. Yes," he said. "Yes, now I see. *That* passage."

What could anyone possibly say about that ludicrous passage? Nothing. But the only way out was through, as Robert Frost, or someone, had once said or written.

"It is," he said, "metaphorical," then looked over at her to see if that sufficed. It did not seem to. He glanced at the audience. Did it suffice for them? They were still blank—bored or angry, he guessed. He couldn't tell which. It could've been both and even a third thing which he couldn't identify.

"We, all of us," he continued, riffing, trying to say many, many words to run out the hour, "carry within us an emptiness, do we not? For I imagine this imagined room, this room I imagined, as empty. That is the salient point here, is it not? Don't you agree? How do we, each of us, move forward with this, our 'empty room,' for lack of a better word, or rather words, for 'empty room' is more than one word, is it not? Don't you agree? I know I do."

He looked over again. She was still waiting for more. He didn't have any more. Against his will, he stole a glance at her lap, pictured his head in it. How peaceful it would be to wait out the hour there, in cozy silence. He couldn't help looking. It was out of his control. Everything was out of his control. He lifted his arm again, just to check. Everyone saw both the lap glance and the arm lift. He was sure of it. On top of it all, he suddenly found himself worried his outfit was feminine, that the attendees would think him a dandy. Did his collar lie too flatly against his shirt? Were its edges unmasculinely rounded? A Peter Pan collar, he believed it to be. Why did he even know this? This brain was someone else's. The Peter Pan collar was introduced by the actress Maude Adams in the 1905 Broadway production of *Peter Pan*. Why did he know *that*? *Peter Pan* by J. M. Barrie. These were the thoughts of another, and of another he didn't like. A coxcomb. Why was he wearing this shirt? Why did he even own it? *Did* he own this shirt? He tried to recall purchasing such a—

"I'm not sure I understand what you're saying," the interviewer said. "Perhaps if you could elabor—"

"Don't you ever feel lonely?" I. spat. "I know I do."

It was the wrong tone, aggressive, but he had had to stop her from talking. She had to stop talking. Everyone had to stop talking. Unfortunately, his tone felt as if he were accusing her, this woman he had only just met, probably, of not being there for him, of not loving him properly, of not welcoming his head into the very lap onto which she had so happily welcomed his book, the book he had written, he might add, his very brain in print, right there on her lap. Why would she so freely welcome his book there—which was his brain in print, was it not?—and not the very head that encased the very brain that wrote that very book?

Oh, he needed someone to love him.

But this wasn't her fault.

It wasn't her responsibility.

He tried to walk his tone back with a smile. He couldn't see his face from inside his head where he found himself situated, nor did he want to, because he was ugly, but he worried this smile on the face part of his head was wrong, too broad and toothy for the reconciliation he had been attempting to communicate. He worried it might appear lecherous instead. He was too old and ugly to look like he was coming on to her. She would be repulsed, justifiably, as would the audience. Then all of them would disperse to share the news of his aged repulsiveness with a vindictive world. And he would be ruined.

"Certainly," she acknowledged, "but—"

"Well, that is your empty room, then. There it is," he said, and bowed.

Bowing was wrong, too. He knew it the moment he did it. It was an instinct but turned out to be a bad one. His instincts were bad. They weren't even *his* instincts. Someone else was pulling the strings. He lifted his arm, almost imperceptibly this time, secretly, just to check again. Everything was wrong.

The interviewer looked at her watch, which he witnessed. He witnessed it! She didn't even try to hide it. What was with her? It seemed unfair, her conspicuous disdain for him. Why did she even take this job if she hated him so much?

"Listen, it's a metaphor, but it's also scientifically sound," he snapped, not meaning to sound snappy, but rather to sound equanimous, if that were a word. He wasn't clear anymore. Equaniminous, perhaps?

"I don't know what you mean," the interviewer said.

"Well, as you do know, we all carry within us neural maps of the various environments we inhabit. For instance, when we close our eyes, we can all picture our homes, their layouts, the placement of our furniture, what have you. That's how we are able to find our way to the bathroom at night, in the dark. Yes? So what I'm suggesting is that the room inside us, were we to examine it, would reveal itself to be a mental configuration of the place in which we live."

He turned to the audience, proudly, tried to curb his instinct to bow once again, failed, and bowed.

"All of you should try it. You'll see. Close your eyes. C'mon, everyone! It's fun!"

I. had no idea if this neural map thing were true. It just came to him, and he said it. It *seemed* true. In any event, no one closed their eyes. They mostly looked down at the floor. The raven-haired Latvian didn't look down; she glared at him. And the interviewer just seemed like she wanted to leave.

"I suppose," she said, "but how does that pertain to your novel?"

"How do you mean?" I. asked, stalling again. "I don't know how you mean." He felt an urge to bring up the eye crumb once more, for sympathy, but wasn't sure it was still pertinent.

"It just seems unlikely to me that I., being homeless, would have a map of a home inside him."

I. had no idea who I. was, other than himself. There was, as far as he knew, no I. in his book, and certainly no homeless person. Everyone in the book had homes. That was a major point of the novel.

"I disagree," he said, flipping through his own copy of the book, forced-casual, only to discover that a character called I. appeared multiple times on nearly every page. He learned, also, that, just as the interviewer had said, I. was homeless.

Oh, come on, he thought.

Then he remembered, in a near panic, the homeless woman in the audience. Would she take offense at his depiction of homelessness, whatever that depiction was? He was no expert in homelessness and would never deign to depict it at all, especially in front of an expert such as herself. He had no idea what he had said about home-lessness in this novel, which didn't seem to be the novel he thought he had written. It could be inaccurate. It was most definitely going to be inaccurate, not to mention offensive, the way the night was going. But, as Robert Frost or someone had advised him, he had to get through this . . . *interrogation*, for that was what this interview had become.

"Well, certainly I. is homeless," he said. "But maybe he wasn't always."

He paused, held his breath, waited for the interviewer to correct him. She looked about to speak but didn't, ob-viously over the whole thing now. So he continued.

"And this is the home I. carries with him, his former home. Although I could argue and do, in a way, that it's this internal room that sustains him, his memory of a better time."

"But doesn't that fly in the face of your just-stated point that the room represents loneliness, if it also rep-resents a better time?"

"Not at all," I. said, without elaboration.

There was a long silence. I. looked out at the crowd again, imploringly. He wasn't sure what he wanted from them. Maybe just a kind nod, a wink of encouragement. No one gave him either. The sailor's eyes were closed. Perhaps he was attempting I.'s experiment. I. instantly felt more warmly toward both him and his outfit.

"You can be alone and have a good time. It's not all bad," he yelled.

The interviewer nodded, studying her notes. She couldn't even look at him anymore.

"The Portuguese have a word for it," he continued. "They call it *sagagiagio*," hoping this were the word, half-remembering reading it on some list of words that had no direct correlation in English.

The interviewer nodded again or maybe she was still nodding from before, still pretending to study her notes.

"So, I'd love to talk a bit about your use of autofiction," she said, now almost inaudible.

"Certainly, all novelists use the raw materials of their lives in their fiction. It is unavoidable, or rather inavoidable, but to characterize that as autofiction seems a bit, well, I mean, just a little, kind of . . . after a fashion . . . as well you know . . . and furthermore . . ." I. trailed off. He had hoped to be interrupted by the interviewer, by the sailor coughing, by anything. But there came only one more terrible silence.

"Still," said the interviewer eventually, "you go so far as to call the protagonist by your own name and include, within the body of the novel, all the information that appears in your author bio on the back cover, not to mention your home address, phone number, and family genealogical chart."

"Listen, it is a literary device. I. is not me. We are

different people. I don't feel the need to defend the practice of autofiction, when I am not practicing it."

"Nor am I asking you to. I simply thought that since
you seem to lean so heavily into this . . . device, with pas-
sages such as: *'There is no difference between I. and me.
There, I said it. I have bled my blood, and with it my very
DNA, onto the page and what results is myself rendered fully
in ink in this very book that rests on your lap. Everything
about I., from his humiliating thoughts to his stilted writing,
seemingly inexplicably in translation, is me. So don't believe
me, if, at some future date, I publicly deny this. The novel
itself is an admission of my guilt.'"*

I. was struck dumb. He hadn't written that. Guilt?
Of what was he supposedly guilty? It wasn't even his
book anymore. It was someone else's guilt. God knows
whose. God knows what was admitted to in it. There
must have been some error at the printers, he suddenly
realised. A mix-up, like babies switched at a hospital.
That kind of thing happened. In fact, he had just read
that very morning about a case of babies switched at
a local hospital. And of a similar case of switched babies at another hospital, some distance away, just last
week. He should have checked the book when it came
out. Why didn't he? But he did, no? He felt certain he
flipped through one of the copies the publisher sent
him. And of what was he guilty, anyway? To what did
he admit?

"It's called autofiction, not autofact," he said triumphantly, this time with no need of a bow.

"Indeed," said the interviewer and then opened it up for questions. There was only one, this from the Latvian.

"Does a woman have a room inside her as well?"

"Yes, of course," he explained. "By 'him,' I meant 'him or her.'"

"Why didn't you write 'him or her,' then?"

"It is understood," I. explained.

"Why must women always be the ones to understand? Why can't you say, 'Everyone carries a room about inside her,' and then men can understand?"

"No one would understand that," I. said.

The raven-haired woman looked him up and down for a long moment and stormed out.

The interviewer thanked I. and thanked the audience for coming.

Three people purchased the novel, which he signed for them in his now unfamiliar loopy cursive at a small, collapsible sighing, or rather signing, table. Not a bad haul, considering. Fifty percent of the audience. The neckerchief woman came up and revealed herself to be his high school girlfriend. He couldn't place her, and her name rang no bell. She reminisced about the time they had attended a Halloween costume party together dressed as a horse. He was the front and had repeatedly passed gas in her face. Everyone at the signing table laughed. I. was humiliated, but certain this had never happened. Anyone who had been in a two-person horse costume would remember it, not to mention remember having repeatedly passed gas within it. If this had happened, he would've awakened hundreds of times in the middle of the night over the years to relive that mortification. He had always been very discreet with his gas passing. In fact, L., his former wife, often said she had not once heard him pass gas in the twenty-odd years of their marriage, an accomplishment of which I. was extremely proud. Neckerchief's story made no sense and, to top it off, after all that, she did not buy one of his books. Why did she even come, this person he couldn't remember, this liar? He packed his bag, shook the interviewer's hand, glanced down at her crotch—damn it!—and was out of the venue onto the street.

Night. Chilly. Crowds of pretty, giant young people cavorting, proud in their giant, cute outfits. This was not their street; it was his. They had not yet been born when he first cavorted on these streets, proud in his own cute, although smaller, outfits. These were his streets by rights, but he was too old to be on them. He was too old to be anywhere. Nothing felt good anymore; nothing felt like anything these days.

He found himself behind the homeless woman pushing a shopping cart piled with her bags. Should he acknowledge her? He thought it proper to, even though she had been at the launch only to get out of the cold. But she was, after all, a person, just like himself, and should be treated as such. This was how we could make the world a better place.

"Thank you for coming to my book launch," he said magnanimously as he passed.

"I've long admired your writing," she said.

He slowed, surprised, pulled a twenty from his wallet, and handed it to her. Immediately, he felt it was the wrong thing to have done. Maybe he should ask for it back, say he hadn't meant to assume she wanted or, more to the point, needed money (because everyone *wanted* money!), that he hadn't meant to insult her, that it was an accident. But there was no comfortable way to do this. Now he was stuck walking next to her. And she walked at a snail's pace (no, snails don't walk; they contract and expand). He guessed that, unlike him, she had nowhere to be. He had somewhere to be—home—and always liked to walk at a clip—he was known for it—however, it seemed rude to just speed off after he had possibly insulted her. So he adjusted his gait, which was torture, and tried to think of something to say.

"I'm glad you like my work," he said. "Do you have a favorite?"

Such a stupid thing to say. *Do you have a favorite? What was he, nine?

"I loved *Drowning in His Soup*," she said. "I don't have

this new one yet, so I can't say if I'd like it more. But it sounds fascinating. I'm glad you tackle the unhoused."

Unhoused! Right, of course, unhoused! He'd been thinking the wrong word all this time. Wasn't that the interviewer's fault, though? Didn't she refer to the un- housed as "homeless"? This was her fault.

"A long time coming in your work," said the unhoused woman, "given how much you write about making the world a better place."

He nodded—did he write about that?—reached into his bag, and pulled out a copy of his book. Maybe he should offer to sell it to her for twenty dollars. That way he could get his twenty back and leave everybody with their dignity. But the book cost twenty-five. Could he ask her for twenty-five dollars? Then he would be taking five dollars from a possibly unhoused person, which didn't seem right. But he didn't want to insult her with a dis- count. It said twenty-five dollars right there on the inside jacket; she would know. He would just give her a copy as a thank-you. It was the only thing to do.

"I can't with complete confidence recommend this book, but I'd like you to have a copy, if you want. As a thank-you."

"Oh! How nice. Could you make it out to I., please?"

"Just like me," I. said, now impossibly exhausted with everything.

"I think that's how I discovered you, because of our names being the same."

I. made the book out to I., handed it to I. I. stuffed it into one of her bags.

"I like how you use the Kafka bit," she said.

"The Kafka bit?"

"The 'room we carry inside' business."

"That's Kafka? Oh! Yes, exactly, Kafka. *Franz* Kafka. I'm impressed you caught that."

"From the Kaiser and Wilkins translation of *The Blue Octavo Notebooks*, right? I'm somewhat disappointed R. didn't know."

"R.?"

"The interviewer."

"Oh! Right. R., yes. The interviewer. Lovely woman, R. Although I had issues with her."

"She clearly hadn't done her homework. You were correct not to hold her hand through the conversation. I liked how you were pranking her by making up some garbage to explain the room. I kept myself from laughing because I didn't want to give away your delectable ruse. But it was brilliant. The idiotic stuff you spouted! Not just then, but through the entire conversation! Completely idiotic! It was a thing of beauty!"

"Thank you," I. said.

Had he been stealing from Kafka? He had never read this *Octaviato whatever whatever*. Had he? He was

certain he had never heard of it. But his memory was going. He understood that much. If this unhoused woman
knew it was from Kafka, someone else would, too. Were
there other stolen things in the book? This was going to
ruin him.

He claimed to have a previous engagement, or rather
an impending engagement, but that it was lovely meeting her, and hurried on ahead, worried that his behind
looked silly as he speed-walked away in his jodhpurs.
It was wrong to leave her, but what was he supposed to
do, spend the entire night with her? She wasn't his date.
Was she? No, almost certainly not. Anyway, he had to
figure out how to deal with the coming accusations of
plagiarism.

Why was he wearing jodhpurs?

And what the hell was *Drowning in His Soup?*

As he hurried home, against his will, I. played over
his interaction with I. It had been all wrong. What
would have been a better, fuller, more humane interaction with this person? He had found himself surprised
at how well-spoken she was, that she had read his previous work or at least work that seemed to have his name
on it. *Drowning in His Soup?* He was ashamed of the
assumptions he had made about her. Out of respect or
penance, he attempted to fully imagine her life, what it
was day to day, where she slept, what dreams she had,
how people treated her. He couldn't. He couldn't even

fully remember how *he* had treated her. He was a failure as a humanitarian.

He arrived at his building to find his key didn't fit in the lock.

Oh.

He tried again. The rain was coming down hard now. He tried it again, peered into the keyhole. Had someone perhaps jammed something in there? A toothpick? A paper clip? A raisin? A crumb? The keyhole seemed clear. He sat on the stoop, flummoxed, soaked. He tried the door again. This made no sense. The café on the corner, his favorite, he suspected, was open until eleven, he believed. He would sit there and dry off. He couldn't think while wet. This had always been the case with him, even as a child.

It was too late to have coffee. So he ordered a slice of carrot cake which featured a cute orange-and-green-icing carrot on top, then checked his bag to see if the copies of his book were soaked. A little damp, but salvageable. He pulled one out. He needed to know what he had written, what he might have to say to defend himself against charges of plagiarism. The book was, he noticed, dedicated to M.

Now and forever. You have made the impossible possible, the unlovable loved, the lost found, the homeless unhoused.

He racked his brain. M? He had known an M. in grade school. A sad, pale boy. Children would pick their

noses and wipe their boogers on his shirt while pretending to pat him on the back in fellowship. Could it be that
M.? They hadn't been close. M. had written a little poem
in I.'s end-of-school-year autograph book, which read:

> *I am not a poit*
> *And I have no fame*
> *But please allow me*
> *To sign my name.*

I. had been upset that M. misspelled *poet*. This had
ruined his entire autograph book. He really wanted to
correct it—simple enough to change the *i* into an *e*—but
he knew that was petty and would be unfair to the purity
of M.'s sentiment, M., who was bullied and covered in
boogers. So he left *poit*. The misspelling haunted I. all
summer. He could never fully forgive M. for ruining his
book. So it was most likely not that M.

He read from Chapter One:

*I. felt out of sorts, foggy and dull, the meat that was his
brain was the wrong meat tonight, not his own meat. Someone else's, perhaps.*

This was not how his book began—his book was
about commercial fishermen—but it wasn't entirely unfamiliar. It felt true somehow, although not precisely in
his voice. He continued:

It was a brain to which he did not have full access. He had some access. He could lift his arm if he wanted, for example, and did, just to prove that he could . . .

Unconsciously, as he read, I. lifted his arm.

. . . but his thoughts were somehow hidden from him. It felt dull in there, in this foreign brain, warm and airless and, somehow, dusty. He imagined watching himself from the outside . . .

I. pictured himself now in this very café, soaking wet, confused, ugly, lifting his arm which was also ugly, but covered, thankfully. A group of attractive young women in crop halters watched him and whispered. He just wanted to go home. Why couldn't he go home? What was happening here? Then, a thought. He flipped through the book until he found his supposed address, phone number and genealogical chart. They weren't his address, phone number, and genealogical chart, but nothing was making sense tonight. He called the phone number. A voice message answered: *We're not able to come to the phone right now. Please leave a message after the tone.*

It sounded like his voice, he thought. He left a message: "It's I. This is a test."

I. made his way through the rain to novel I.'s address. There, his key easily turned the front-door lock, and he made his way to I.'s apartment, where the other key on his ring easily turned that lock.

The apartment was empty, as if no one lived there. A single room, warm and airless and dusty, with a mirror

fastened to one wall. As I. stepped inside, the mirror rattled. He found himself staring for a bit out one of the
two windows into the night, at the rain. He discovered
he liked the emptiness of the place. His other apartment,
his real apartment, was stuffed with memories, all the
furniture and doodads and books, artefacts of a sad marriage and all the terrible mistakes he had made, the bur-
dens he had buckled under. This new place wasn't exactly
a fresh start, as the paint was peeling and it was dirty
and smelled of mildew, but it was without those constant
reminders. The answering machine on the floor next to
the phone was blinking. He pressed the playback button.

"It's E. This is a test."

He was fairly certain that was not what he said earlier. It seemed unlike him, contrary to his philosophy of
life, and a bit hysterical. Nothing is a test, he always said,
because if it is, then who exactly is the quizmaster? This
usually shut people up. And wasn't his name I.? Why did
the answering machine say "E."? In any event, now that
he was beginning to dry off, he could think more clearly.
It was a nice place, nicer than his previous one. He would
order a bed in the morning. Maybe some saucepans and
cutlery. But would he? Could he? This wasn't his apartment. It was becoming difficult to keep his thinking
straight, even though he was now fully dry. The keys
worked here. The keys didn't work at the other apartment. This was the address he had listed in his book. But

wasn't that just fiction, even if it were of the auto variety?
Clearly he was not unhoused, as was the I. in the book.
Or was it E. who was unhoused? Wait, was the unhoused
E. of the book the unhoused woman he met tonight? But
the E. in the book was male. He looked down at the pe-
nis hanging between his legs. When had he removed his
clothes? To dry off? He couldn't recall, and moved from
the window, ashamed of his nakedness. Granted, gender is fluid, he mused as he slipped back into his underwear—was this his underwear? It seemed different. Did
his have so many buttons and zippers?—and sat on the
couch—was there a couch before?—opened the novel—
which was now called *Bebop Botox Blues*—to a random
page and attempted to read. He couldn't focus, as his
underwear was off again and the gray velvet upholstery,
warm and soft on his balls, titillated him. Then, a moment of panicked clarity: whose couch was this, really?
Who sat on it naked before him? With whose possibly
diseased genitalia was his genitalia now comingling? But
then against his will he relaxed, settled into the velvet
and felt, perhaps for the first time in his life, adventurous
and whole. He read:

*E., luxuriating nakedly on her new velvet couch, finally
out of the weather, read from the novel that the elderly author
had sold her for twenty dollars. "Things change suddenly,
inexplicably. One day a dark spot appears on your skin. Or
was it always there? Or did it appear gradually, darkening*

over time, like the gradual darkening of night, only you didn't notice it at first, because you weren't paying attention, because you didn't take the time to look, and then one day the spot was so dark that it had become impossible to miss. The conservation of matter tells us the dark spot has always existed somewhere in the universe in some form. This can be comforting if you don't consider that in its present form it might foretell your death."

E. looked up from the passage. Another bit he did not remember writing. He was going to be in terrible trouble if this, too, was stolen. And they knew where to find him, the authorities. The book would lead them to him. Plagiarism was a crime. He knew this because he'd researched it for this novel, or at least the version he thought he'd written, the one about the commercial fisherman who moonlighted—or rather moonlit—as a plagiarist. One could be fined up to a quarter of a million dollars for plagiarism. One could be sentenced to prison for up to ten years for plagiarism. E.'s protagonist, Saunders Mucklebackit, had been accused of it by Santiago, another fisherman author, who claimed Mucklebackit had stolen his work, then aged his version of the manuscript with tea to make the paper appear older than Santiago's.

Anyway, what creature, if not a shark, *does* look for weakness and then pounce, E. wondered. Man! Of course! Or, rather, *human*, so as not to offend that Latvian woman.

The sound of a key in the lock.

The apartment door swung open to reveal the Latvian woman.

Oh.

She and E. regarded each other silently, suspiciously.

"E." She nodded, then stepped in, closed the door, crossed to the abattoir, or rather the armoire, opened it, wriggled out of her soaking Latvian dress, which she left in a pile on the floor as she donned her robe. Had there been an abattoir—or rather armoire—there previously? He couldn't recall. The Latvian opened a window, lit a cigarette, stared out at the rain. E. knew he had to say something, but what? What could he say to this stranger?

"How was the *Gatves deja* tonight?"

"It was fine. Whatever. I lost my *trīdeksnis*. I looked like an idiot, shaking my empty hand."

It wasn't the first time she had lost her *trīdeksnis*, and E. found himself utilizing his neural map, going through all the places she might have left it: on the bookcase, behind the newspapers piled on the desk, in the cabinet under the television. He thought he might've seen it there earlier and he headed toward the TV.

"Just . . . don't look for it now. Please," she said irritably. "There's no point. I don't need it now."

He stopped, sighed.

"Please don't be mad about the passage," he said.

She remained silent for a bit, dragged on her cigarette.

"You knew how I felt," she said.

And she was right; he did. How, though? How any of this?

"But here's the thing: gender is fluid," he said.

"What does that even mean in this context?"

"'Gender is fluid' means something in every context. I thought we agreed on that. Besides, I just found out I didn't even write the damn thing."

"The passage?"

"Apparently, I stole it. From Kafka."

"You never told me you stole it from Kafka. You never tell me anything."

Her eyes welled up.

"Nothing in this this book is familiar. Although it's becoming more familiar as I have been reading it tonight. I can't tell if that's because I remember writing it or am remembering reading it tonight."

"We've been arguing about that goddamn passage for two years," she said, and seemed heartbroken.

He found a tomato on the kitchenette counter. Bright red, shiny, perfect. There was no other food in the apartment. He cut it open with the only knife there, silver, sharp, shiny, perfect. Inside, the tomato was white and hard, solid with the vague imprint of the inside of a tomato. It was nauseating.

"The tomato has gone bad," he said.

"It's that terrible market," she said, somewhat dreamily.

"This city is filled with terrible markets. What can a woman do? And by woman, I mean person."

"I wonder if I should eat it anyway."

"If it's brown, put it down. If it's red, go ahead."

"It's white."

"If it's white, take a bite."

He did; spat it out.

"The consistency of grout."

"Tastes like grout? Spit it out."

"I did."

"Good boy."

And he felt proud. He realized he loved her and had for a very long time. She was, of course, M. His M., M. who made the unlovable lovable.

The telephone rang. M. looked over. E. stared at it, now atop a small-size table, or rather a small side table. He knew he had to answer but couldn't. He did.

"Hello?"

"I found this number in your novel," the voice said.

"Yes?"

"I'm the broad-shouldered tough in a tan sports jacket."

"Okay."

"I was in the audience for your book launch earlier. I may be an undercover policeman."

"Yes."

There was a silence.

"Can I help you?" E. said.

"I've been reading your book. I bought a copy after, as you may recall."

"Yes. I recall. Of course I recall."

Another long silence. E. found himself frightened.

"The book raises questions."

"What do you mean?"

"The things you admit to are extremely—"

"It is autofiction," E. interrupted. "Emphasis on 'fiction,' mister."

"Yes," said the man. "Still, there are things only the perpetrator would know."

More silence as E. gathered his courage.

"Perpetrator of what?"

But there was just a dial tone.

E. stood there, holding the receiver. M. watched from the couch.

"Come," she said. "Rest your head in my lap."

There was nothing E. wanted more, but he had to read, had to find out what he had admitted to.

"Can I read the book with my head in your lap?"

"Lay your head, close your eyes. I'll read it to you."

E. hung up the phone and, with gratitude, made his way to her.

M. read.

I am soaked, wandering the streets. Simply by existing I have caused damage. I have tried to change. I have changed, but it doesn't make it better. It has been said by men wiser than I that one cannot live without killing. I haven't wanted to kill. I consider myself peaceful, peace-loving. I have tried to be kind, but even in my clumsy attempts at kindness I have caused pain.

"Does it really say that?"

"Is it untrue?"

"It's starting to sound familiar. Keep reading."

"I'll change," I cry. "I'll change. But the one thing I can't change, or rather don't, is that I don't tell anyone who I really am. I want to be alive, to be free, but I know that I am uranium and, for the good of all, I must stay within the lead casing that is my skull. I've always known this, or at least for as long as I can recall. And I recall encouraging others to paint pretty, colorful pictures on my lead casing, which I display with pride."

E. looked around the room, his home, his prison. The split tomato sat on the counter surrounded now by a box of pasta, a lemon, an open bag of pistachios. The drawers were full of cutlery, the cabinets piled with dishes that had been dirtied and washed and dirtied and washed and dirtied and washed a thousand times. He knew this without opening the cabinets, without lifting his head from M.'s lap as she read to him from the novel he had written. The bookshelves—some of the books there he had read, most he had not. *The Blue Octavo Notebooks* was there. He knew that passage was underlined. He remembered his familiar loopy scribble in the margin. "Use this!" it read.

M. continued reading, her voice swam around E., describing leisurely curlicues. The story shifted and shifted again. It shimmered, turned inside out, the words meaning something new and then meaning nothing, as E. walked through a field of junked cars. A man in a blue T-shirt carried a too-long ladder. Afraid, E. jumped into a rusted car, one so small he had to sit crouched. Sky darkened. Rain? No, just night arriving. Blinded by darkness, the man with the ladder banged it clumsily against various cars. The banging got closer. If he banged the ladder against E.'s car, I. would die. It was a superstitious game E. played, but it was also true. He squinted into the blackness, searching for the ladder man, shoving greasy fast food from a paper bag into his mouth. The car was now moving, slowly, and the black night became a darkened basement. A party. Sailor was there, with a drawn-on mustache. Effete young man in his beret was there, also with a mustache, but his made of hair. Crowd parted as the car pushed through. Then E. passed gas again and again, looked behind to see neckerchief in the back seat, a teenager here, but at the same time fifty, disgusted. Humiliated, E. climbed from the car, which had become a horse costume, ran up the stairs, out of the house. Was he galloping? He could never go back.

E. awoke mortified, having relived that high school horse costume incident in his dream, just as he had awakened mortified about it hundreds of times in the past.

What a waste of mortification, he realized, judging by the reaction of the small audience present and then gone. Nothing. A fart. Yet he couldn't shake the feeling. L., his high school girlfriend, had smelled the shameful stench that came from within him. His life had been hiding. He stared at the ceiling.

M. was gone and the room was empty. He knew she and the furnishings would return and be gone again. Sometimes they would arrive as shadows, sometimes as if he could touch them. He knew the mistakes he carried in this life were no easier to carry than the ones from the other. He knew he both loved M. and had never seen her before tonight. He knew he had been I. before E. and would be I. again. Then E., then I., then E., then I.

Oh.

The mirror rattled once again, offering itself, as he tiptoed to the open window. Outside was black, but it wasn't night that made it so. He felt an intense heat, smelled blood, smelled flesh.

He could lift his arm to touch this wall of meat pressing into the room, but he didn't.

CONTRIBUTORS' BIOS

NAOMI ALDERMAN is the bestselling author of *The Future* and *The Power*, which won the Women's Prize for Fiction, was chosen as a book of the year by the *New York Times*, the *Washington Post*, the *Los Angeles Times*, and was recommended as a book of the year by both Barack Obama and Bill Gates. *The Power* was recently adapted as a series for Amazon Prime. As a novelist, Alderman has been mentored by Margaret Atwood via the Rolex Arts Initiative, she is a Fellow of the Royal Society of Literature, and her work has been translated into more than thirty-five languages. As a video games designer, she was lead writer on the groundbreaking alternate reality game Perplex City, and is co-creator of the award-winning smartphone exercise adventure game Zombies, Run!, which has more than 10 million players. She lives in London.

ELIF BATUMAN's first novel, *The Idiot*, was a finalist for the Pulitzer Prize and for the Women's Prize. The sequel, *Either/Or*, was published in 2022. She has been a staff writer at *The New Yorker* since 2010.

JOSHUA COHEN's books include the novels *Moving Kings, Book of Numbers, Witz, A Heaven of Others*, and *Cadenza for the Schneidermann Violin Concerto*; the short-fiction collection *Four New Messages*, and the nonfiction collection *Attention: Dispatches from a Land of Distraction*. Cohen was awarded Israel's 2013 Matanel Prize for Jewish Writers, and in 2017 was named one of *Granta*'s Best Young American Novelists. His most recent novel, *The Netanyahus*, won the National Jewish Book Award for Fiction and the Pulitzer Prize for Fiction. He lives in New York City.

CHARLIE KAUFMAN is the writer of a story in this collection.

YIYUN LI is the author of eleven books, including *Wednesday's Child*; *The Book of Goose*, which received the PEN/Faulkner Award; *Where Reasons End*, which received the PEN/Jean Stein Book Award; the memoir *Dear Friend, from My Life I Write to You in Your Life*; and the novels *The Vagrants* and *Must I Go*. She is the recipient of a MacArthur Fellowship, Guggenheim Fellowship, Windham-Campbell Prize, PEN/Malamud Award, and PEN/Hemingway Award. She teaches at Princeton University.

TOMMY ORANGE is the *New York Times* bestselling author of *Wandering Stars* and *There There*, which was a finalist for the Pulitzer Prize and winner of the 2018 Center for Fiction First Novel Prize. *There There* was long-listed for the National Book Award for Fiction in 2018, the Aspen Words Literary Prize, and the Carnegie Medal for Excellence in Fiction in 2019. It was deemed a Top Five Fiction Book of the Year by the *New York Times* and won the John Leonard Award for Best First Book and the PEN/Hemingway Award for Debut Novel.

HELEN OYEYEMI's books include *What Is Not Yours Is Not Yours*, *Gingerbread*, and *Parasol Against the Axe*. She's a recipient of the Somerset Maugham Award and PEN's Open Book Award, and her novel *Peaces* was short-listed for the Goldsmiths Prize.

KEITH RIDGWAY is from Dublin. He is the author of *A Shock*, which was awarded the James Tait Black Memorial Prize; *Hawthorn & Child*; and *Animals*. He has been awarded the Prix Femina Étranger in France and the Rooney Prize for Irish Literature. He lives in south London.

LEONE ROSS is a novelist, short story writer, editor, and educator. Her third novel, *This One Sky Day*, was nominated for the Women's Prize, the Goldsmiths Prize, and the Ondaatje Prize, among other honors—and named a *New York Times* Editor's Choice. Her short fiction has been widely anthologized and her first short-story collection, *Come Let Us Sing Anyway*, prompted the *Times Literary Supplement* to call her "a pointilliste, a master of detail." In 2021, she won the Manchester Prize for Fiction for a single short story. Ross has taught creative writing for twenty-five years, and worked as a journalist throughout the 1990s. She is the editor of *Glimpse: A Black British Anthology of Speculative Fiction*, published in 2022.

BECCA ROTHFELD is an essayist, critic, editor, and philosopher, and the author of *All Things Are Too Small*. She has written for publications such as the *New York Review of Books*, the *Times Literary Supplement*, the *New Yorker*, the *Atlantic*, and the *New York Times Book Review*, and she is currently the nonfiction book critic at the *Washington Post* and an editor at *The Point*. She lives in Washington, DC, with her husband and her dog, Kafka.

ALI SMITH was born in Inverness and lives in Cambridge. Her fiction has been translated into more than forty languages.

LINES WRITTEN BY KAFKA

"A Cage Went in Search of a Bird," "The history of mankind is the instant between two strides taken by a traveller," and "If it had been possible to build the Tower of Babel without climbing it, it would have been permitted" are all taken from *The Third Octavo Notebook*, in *The Blue Octavo Notebooks*, translated by Ernst Kaiser and Eithne Wilkins.

"Everyone carries a room about inside him. This fact can even be proved by means of the sense of hearing. If someone walks fast and one pricks up ones ears and listens, say in the night, when everything round about is quiet, one hears, for instance, the rattling of a mirror not quite firmly fastened to the wall" is taken from *The First Octavo Notebook*, in *The Blue Octavo Notebooks*.

Quotations in the introduction are taken from Franz Kafka, *The Zürau Aphorisms*, translated by Michael Cage Hofmann and Geoffrey Brock, with an introduction and afterword by Roberto Calasso, published by Schocken in 2006.

With thanks to the Oxford Kafka Research Centre and the AHRC project Kafka's Transformative Communities.